"I must go,"

Alianora insisted, but the viscount barred her way.

"Wait. Please. Perhaps it is time we spoke sensibly to one another."

She clutched her reticule. "I cannot think what we might say."

"I can think of many things." Cerestone stepped closer. "Friends may speak to one another at any time, on any subject. Friends trust one another."

Words failed her. She could not move.

"Alianora." He said her name as if it were music. "I wish to apologize. It was difficult to see you in the clutches of that villain. I should have realized that you would never willingly consent to be his wife."

Her eyes flew to his. Had he guessed? Did he know?

"Only give me the right and I shall protect you," he begged.

"I cannot."

He was so close now that she could smell the light scent of his cologne.

"Then tell me that you love him, that you desire his touch above all others, that you would beg him to do this—" He began to kiss her neck, moving gently but relentlessly to her ear, her cheek. "And this," he whispered huskily as he bent to kiss her lips . . .

Maid of Honor

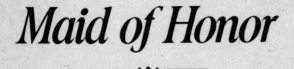

Stephanie Spearman

PAGEANT BOOKS

♪

PAGEANT BOOKS
225 Park Avenue South
New York, New York 10003

PAGEANT and colophon are trademarks of the publisher

Cover artwork by Franco Accornero

Printed in the U.S.A.

First Pageant Books printing: February, 1989

10 9 8 7 6 5 4 3 2 1

To Charlie, for supporting my Regency habits

Maid of Honor

Chapter One

It was a fine misty morning in Kent that saw three friends on the road to London. Their carriage traveled at a jaunty pace along the Medway, followed by a luggage-laden fourgon. Two of the trio lazily watched the passing scenery while the third snored rather enthusiastically, oblivious to his surroundings. Seven hours would see them at their destination; eight hours would see them at White's settling in for a long night of play. But such complacency simply begged to be overset, and, in this particular instance, a loud brassy arpeggio announced the interruption.

"That sound!" Buck Rasherly observed.

"Rather like a yard-of-tin orchestra," commented Peter Everhurst, Viscount Cerestone, with a small smile.

"The fox!" cried Henry Parkington, coming awake. He glanced confusedly about the carriage. Then, seeing he was not on the hunting field, he fell back against the velvet squabs and began to snore loudly once more.

"And there it is again. How odd," said Buck. "Horns of some sort." He lifted his quizzing glass and focused a magnified gray eye on Parkington. "Although one can hardly hear it over the noise in this carriage."

Cerestone laughed, amusement softening what was a rather severe face in repose. His green eyes twinkled. "We should be able to see something once we climb above the river."

"Ah, this wretched mist," Buck lamented. Indeed, the mist presented an appalling threat to his carefully arranged dark locks.

"You mean this wretched morning."

"That too, dear boy. What folly to play at cards the entire night when we might have been sleeping."

"Rather, what folly to sleep when we might have been at cards," Cerestone corrected. As he lifted a dark brow, Buck nodded.

"Quite so." He turned stiffly to the carriage window, admirably avoiding the shirt points that threatened his eyes. "Why, Cerestone, I do believe we are climbing."

"It is inevitable in the Downs." Cerestone opened the guidebook that had been lying idle in his hands. He leafed through it, searching for the section on the Medway Valley. Already this morning he had forced his friends to pause in Aylesford so that they might admire the numerous red-tiled roofs, the lovely old church above High Street surrounded by elms just beginning to put forth their reddish flower clusters, and the friary, built of mellow-golden ragstone, once inhabited by Carmelite monks.

Admittedly, both Buck and Henry had been less than enthralled with his historical obsession but surprised Cerestone and themselves by waxing enthusiastic about the next stop: a prehistoric tomb called Kits Coty House. This site presented the opportunity for a wager. Everyone knew that witches had built the thing, but who was inside? After a half hour of speculation, Cerestone had had to drag his friends away.

"Surely there is nothing left to see in this valley," Buck protested, looking askance.

"There might be," the viscount answered hopefully, holding the pages up to the light. "Why, look here!"

Buck moaned softly.

"Castle ruins! Real ones, not Gothic follies. We are quite near them in fact."

The moan rose in volume.

"Grassmere, built 1374 to enable Edward III to control river traffic—"

"It excites me," Buck ended with a sigh.

"As well it should," the viscount told him with a chuckle, closing the guidebook. "However, I shall not subject you to further historical torture as the ruins are on the east bank and we are on the west."

"A reprieve, by Jove!"

"Take note, my friend, that it is only because I intend to arrive in London and open the house before my stepmother arrives. She does like her comfort." He put the guidebook away in his leather satchel, squeezing it in among papers, pens, inkwells, and other books.

"I remember all too well, dear boy. We were three 'horrid little boys' when we disturbed her peace at Woodhurst."

No, Cerestone thought ruefully, the dowager Lady Cerestone had never appreciated him and his two fellow Harrovians playing banshee about the house during their holidays. It had invariably led to a nervous attack on the part of his stepmama, which led to either a stern word from the old viscount, or, if the behavior was truly outrageous, The Strap.

"And how is your stepsister Georgy?" Buck asked, pursing his lips. "I recall she was quite an avid follower—but cried when her dresses got muddy."

"She is grown up—you wouldn't know her—and impatient to be fired off," Cerestone told him.

"And, it seems," Buck said, his gray, myopic eyes looking amused, "Lady Cerestone plans to fire *you* off."

The viscount groaned. Since the death of her husband five years earlier, Lady Cerestone had secluded herself at Woodhurst, but lately had announced her wish to return to an active life in town. She intended to join the London season already underway, to launch her older daughter, and to find her stepson a bride—a fashionable young lady who would be adept at running a household and who would have the proper understanding and compassion for a mother-in-law's sensibilities.

That was when he had thought of his school chums. He wrote to them, begging that they remember the pact made at Harrow: that the three of them would support each other through the nasty vicissitudes of life, which included, at the time, some bullying upperclassmen. Now he would need their aid in thwarting the dowager's plans; he hoped at the same time that they might indulge in some play of their own. Then Cerestone wished nothing more than to return to Woodhurst unwed and continue with his research and writing. There was time later to think of marrying—he was only thirty, after all!

But only yesterday, while visiting Henry at his estate south of Maidstone, Cerestone's valet-fellow bibliophile, Trench, had said, "If I knows the mistress, my lord, you'll come home neatly wrapped and done to a turn. You'll be jumpin' the broom before summer."

"You are wrong," the viscount told him then added desperately, "there will be three of us."

Trench tapped one of the Gothic romances he carried in his coat pocket and nodded wisely.

"Three won't do. A hundred won't do. I've read about this time and again."

"Life is not a Gothic romance, Trench—more like a picaresque novel if one is not careful."

"And you intend to write your own fate, my lord? I'll bet my fine caracalla wig on your losing."

Trench's guffaw still echoed in Cerestone's mind as he told Buck, "Between you and my own determination, I will survive the Season unshackled."

"We will be a bulwark against all aspiring mamas. First, however, we must see to Henry." Buck turned his quizzing glass on the sleeping bulk across from them. "He dresses like a country squire."

"He is a country squire."

"But one need not advertise the fact. One never wears a suit of a single color. The coat, waistcoat, and nether integuments must be of differing colors and differing materials."

Henry indeed wore all brown worsted—a suit of dittos. With a lock of straight brown hair falling across his forehead, his long chin, and brown suit, he looked quite like one of his chestnut horses. His snores even ended on a whinny once in a while.

All this made Cerestone very self-conscious, more so when Buck turned the quizzing glass on him. He tugged at the sleeve of his coat, a parsley green corduroy with shiny elbows. He wore comfortable breeches, softened, old top boots, and a less than pristine shirt. Buck had always had the knack of looking at ease in the tight, fashionable clothes, but Peter had chosen comfort and Henry had never cared. Among the beau monde Buck had already earned the nickname "The Walking Stick" due to his high sense of de rigueur and slender proportions.

The quizzing glass continued to stare. "You have been too long in the country, dear boy; however, I shall exert myself to see you both brought up to the mark."

"I think I appreciate your concern."

"You shall," Buck assured him. "You would not wish to embarrass Georgy."

Peter laughed a little. "To Georgy I am a raw bookworm who can only turn into a moth—never a socially acceptable butterfly."

"Young ladies just coming on the town wish all aspects to be perfect," Buck said knowledgeably. "They are forever afraid of a beau crying off because his future brother-in-law's shirt points were too low."

"Yes, you survived the debut of your sister, did you not?"

"Most excruciating experience of my life."

"How, uh, auspicious."

"Not to fear, dear boy. Everyone survives. And you shall have my experience to call upon."

"So kind." The viscount chuckled and leaned back against the squabs, stretching his long legs as much as he could, then closed his eyes.

Not for long, however. A loud snort of horns woke them all again, but this time it was more musical: a fanfare, a third brassy arpeggio.

Henry came awake grumbling. "Wish them all at Jericho," he insisted. "With that off-wheeler, kicks, can feel it in my feet."

The viscount looked through the coach's misty window and caught a glimpse of something across the river through the dissipating fog. He blinked rapidly, shook his head, then quickly lowered the carriage glass. "Hal, look! Tell me you don't see horses down there."

Henry leaned forward. What he saw caused him to become so animated that if he had been a smaller man he would almost have fallen out the window, but as only either end and not the middle would ever have fit through the tiny square, neither of the other two men was particularly concerned.

"I do say!" Henry exclaimed.

Buck refused to look, maintaining for the moment his exquisite poise. "Would one of you be so good as to explain the nature of that odd sound?" he asked without betraying an ounce of curiosity.

Rather than answering, Cerestone rapped on the roof for the coachman to stop. Before the footman could let down the steps, he had jumped from the coach and made his way to the crest of a small hill, crushing dandelions and cow parsley and tall grass in his rush. He did not notice the beautiful spring leaves of the sparse beechwoods or the white blossoms of the cherry trees or the greenish flowers of the laurel or the tiny yellow flowers of the dogs mercury hiding in the shade. Nor did he hear the plaintive call of the robin, the beautiful fluting of the blackbird. He saw and heard only what was across the water.

There was a rather sharp bend in the river, a narrow point. When the fourgon carrying all their luggage caught them up, the viscount ordered Trench to fetch his spy glass.

"Have you ever seen the like?" Cerestone asked softly as he held the glass to his eye. "It must be the ruins of Old Grassmere."

"Still ain't sure I ain't dreamin'," Henry said. "Horses. Destriers."

Cerestone looked at him in surprise. "Why, yes, they are destriers. How'd you know that?"

"A horse, ain't it?" Henry returned, nodding.

"It would be inherently good of one of you to describe what is so devastatingly marvelous," Buck complained. "A quizzing glass only sees so far."

"Buck," Henry said, heartily clapping him on the shoulder, " 'tis a game of knights and horses."

"Chess?" the dandy asked in disbelief, brushing off his jacket.

"A joust," the viscount supplied.

"Is that not, as one might say, *medieval?*" Buck asked in disbelief.

"Exactly." Cerestone's green eyes fairly danced. "Complete with keep, pennants, pavilions, and knights." The ruins of Old Grassmere sat on an island in the silvery river—bailey and motte, a castle and curtain wall surrounding and occupying an artificial hill. The inner keep where the family would have lived was relatively untouched by time, lacking only a roof; the outer keep remained as only a few feet of wall. Of other buildings—what might have been a barracks, mews for falconry, stables, kitchens—only a few telling stones lay about in the tall grass. Cerestone could see a road, built up and well kept, leading from the island to the other side of the river. At one time the castle would have been protected by a drawbridge, but he saw no evidence of one.

Two knights—one dressed in a blue and gold jupon over his armor, the other dressed in white with the red cross of St. George on his breast—lifted wooden lances held securely beneath their elbows and maneuvered decorated shields. Sunlight flashed off the polished helmets as the knights charged. Cerestone held his breath. The lances crossed the tilt—a fence covered with maroon velvet that separated the two horses. The blunted end of one lance slipped under the shield of the knight of St. George. The knight fell back in his tall saddle, feet and lance flying up as he toppled off the horse and landed with a thump on the hard ground.

Cerestone winced. Servants dressed as pages and squires rushed from a pavilion to the fallen knight and helped him to his feet. He sighed. The knight seemed to be unhurt.

He moved his glass to the royal loges, describing to Henry and Buck what he had just witnessed and what he saw now: a man dressed in kingly robes, a golden crown encircling his brow; a woman by him in red also wearing a crown. The woman stood up and beckoned the fallen knight to her. He obeyed, almost reluctantly, removing his helmet. She leaned out of the loge, touched him about the head, then sat down, apparently satisfied.

A number of women sat behind the man and woman; a flock of colors—green, blue, purple, yel-

low costumes—topped by pointedly exotic head-
dresses trailing windblown wisps of gauze. His glass
stopped on a young girl. She wore an overgown of
turquoise, a tight-sleeved undergown of canary yellow, a chaplet of flowers on her head from which
depended many bright ribbons. Rising as two
knights on their destriers (which Henry explained
were not true destriers but more likely the huge
Suffolk Punches used as plowhorses, recruited and
trained for the joust) came to the stands, the girl
pulled some ribbons from her headdress and from
her braids, thick flaxen plaits that hung to her waist,
and tied the ribbons to the lances of the knights.

"Wynyate!" Henry suddenly exclaimed as he borrowed the viscount's spy glass. "Knew I'd remember 'em. Strange earl. Obsessed with ancestors.
Rode with one of the Edwards. Ancestor, I mean."
He handed the glass back, but Buck intercepted it
with an incredibly fast movement and had a look at
the scene.

"Spring Tourney," Henry continued in his halt-
forward style of speaking. "Saint George's Day."

"So it is," the viscount agreed. "I remember the
name now. Wynyate. It was mentioned in the
guidebook."

"Saw it once as a child. Don't remember much."

"Who is the young girl with the pale hair?" Cerestone felt such a desire to be there among them,
celebrating history, an experience far different from
reading about it.

"Alianora," Henry said, finally remembering. He
retrieved the spy glass from Buck and fixed it to his
left eye. "Quiet sort. Played some medieval harp."

"How old is she? Couldn't be more than fifteen,"
the viscount observed.

Henry frowned, handing the glass to Cerestone, dancing it around Buck's insistent fingers. "Nineteen if she's a day. Youngest boy's at Oxford." He looked back at the coach, noticed the postilion was off the leader leaning against a tree. With a whistle he ordered the boy back to keep an eye on the cattle. Then he turned to Cerestone. "Been sent down. Heard of it. Painted some statuary."

"Ah," said Buck. "We, my dear boy, were a bit more creative in our time."

"So we were," the viscount mused.

Buck harumphed elegantly and leaned stiffly toward Henry. "The time we nailed the library furniture to the ceiling," he said.

"Never caught," Henry responded, rubbing his thumbs under his brown velvet lapels.

Buck continued his reminiscence, warming to the subject. "And that marvelous time we carved our names on the keystone. Quite neat, I do say."

"Got caught," Henry said, thumbs dropping to his pockets.

"No question of who perpetrated that," Cerestone added.

"And that delicious forgery allowing us to visit the old tavern."

"You certainly were a complete hand, Buck."

Buck preened. Henry snorted inelegantly.

"And"—Buck held up his gloved hand—"our most magnificent—"

"Bull!" Henry expelled.

Buck glared at him.

"Why, yes," Cerestone said, lowering the glass. "Putting that toothless old bull in the headmaster's office."

"Almost sent down," Henry choked.

"But he gladly allowed us to graduate instead," the viscount observed.

A roar from the crowd across the river recaptured their attention.

"What's to?" Henry demanded. The viscount handed him the glass.

"By Jove, knocked him flat. Good show. Gad, wish I could be there. Ain't there a bridge across this demmed river?"

Cerestone chuckled. "We passed one several miles back."

"No!" Buck planted his ivory walking stick most emphatically into the dandelions by his gleaming Hessians. "I most certainly will not turn back, not at this juncture. We should never reach London in time for supper." Despite his appearance, Buck could delicately wolf down more food than Henry and drink more bottles of port than most of London. A six bottle man. Cerestone had always admired that. So had Henry in a begrudging way.

Henry looked up at the thin baron's son. "Can't think of anything but food," he observed in disgust.

Buck aimed his quizzing glass meaningfully at Henry's expanding waistcoat.

The viscount took back the spy glass and gazed once more at the medieval scene, focusing on the girl, Alianora. She was seated on a stone bench now. He watched a knight who had just won a joust beg a favor of her. His lips tightened when he made out who it was: Richard Brendall, Earl of Savernake, a notorious fortune hunter. Last year, he had dared to try for his sister, Georgina, luring her from the ladies' seminary with charm and promises. The schoolmistress caught her leaving and reported it to the viscount, who brought Georgina back to Woodhurst and let her finish her studies with her old governess. As yet, she had not completely forgiven him.

"The queen of love and beauty," he mumbled to himself. The most beautiful woman in medieval lore, to whom the knights owed homage. Even from this distance he could see that the knight, Savernake, had asked something that disturbed her. After a moment of confusion, hands held up in refusal, she finally assented. She picked up a stringed instrument beside her on the bench. It looked something like a small harp, but he wasn't quite certain from this distance. It was now obvious the winning knight had asked the favor of a song. After plucking a few strings, she began to sing, bowing her head at first, then looking up. He could hear her faintly, a high, clear sound on the breeze. He lowered the glass.

"Time fleets," Buck reminded him, picking up one watch fob then another, shaking his head, and looking further until he at last found his true watch.

Cerestone looked innocent. "Why, Buck, don't you paint a red dot on the real fob?"

Buck snapped the cover shut. "A red dot? A *red dot?*" He became quite incoherent after that with words surfacing such as ignorant, faux fobs, and setting the fashion.

"Well, it is true I have much to learn about life in town," the viscount admitted, a twinkle in his eye. He turned to look one last time across the river.

Henry put a hand on Peter's shoulder. "Never do, you know."

Startled, Cerestone asked, "What won't do?"

"The Wynyate gal. Old earl's too queer by half. No doubt want a knight of the Round Table for her."

A light of challenge flickered across the viscount's face. "I should merely like to meet her sometime, and meet her father, certainly. Purely a scholarly exercise."

"Then I suggest you outfit yourself as a knight and attend the tourney," Buck suggested as if it were quite that simple.

"Perhaps I will. Sometime."

Buck waved his quizzing glass, one of the hundreds in his collection. Today's glass was set in a teakwood handle, the end carved to resemble an elephant holding the ribbon in its trunk. "Never, dear Parkington, underestimate our friend Cerestone. You forget the innumerable troubles he could foment and yet escape smelling of violets."

Henry snorted. "Mean roses."

"Violets, dear boy, are for innocence."

"Aye. You did some pretty deeds too, *dear boy*. Before you was such an exquisite, that is."

Buck squawked. *"Never* call me that. It informs the world of your ignorance. Aside from that, however, it is far pleasanter to be named 'exquisite' than to smell like a stable. Oh," he said faintly, pulling a lacy lavender-scented handkerchief from inside his sleeve and waving it about his face, "at times the odor is overwhelming."

"Better than the Frog water you pour on," Henry complained.

"French," Buck insisted. "Eau de cologne. My dear boy, even Boney requires several bottles a day."

"Recommends it, certainly."

Cerestone laughed. "Ah, Parkington, you must learn all these things to rub along well in society."

"Don't want to rub along. Horses are more interesting." He then turned to check the horses once again and snorted. "Demmed post-boys, kept the cattle standing all this time." He walked briskly toward the postilion who now sat on the off-leader, staring absently into the distance with his arms folded across his chest. Henry gave the boy a few sharp instructions in how to handle horses kept idling after a fast trot, then climbed into the carriage. The postilion grimaced at Henry's back, pulled his cap down over his forehead, and returned to his contemplation.

"A true boor," Buck observed as they began to walk back to the carriage.

"I thought he was a horse," Cerestone said thoughtfully.

"That too," Buck observed.

"Ah, but he would ever stand by you, loyal and steadfast as any *mount.*"

"One could be *hacked* to death."

"Or *cobbled.*"

"Only if it were to become a *hobby.*"

"Nothing so *palfrey* as that," the viscount returned sedately.

"Or so *prad*-ical."

"But it could send one *gambaldynge* through the thistles."

Buck remained silent a moment then reluctantly dug into a waistcoat pocket and handed his friend a Roman coin. Who had found the coin originally no one recalled, but it had always been held by the winner of their wit war. Buck had won the last encounter.

Cerestone smiled. "You almost had me again until I remembered my medieval history and the sorts of horses that were popular then. But then, you were the best in our form at school."

Buck nodded. "Yes. I was."

"And Parkington was the embodiment of a pugilist."

"So he was. I remember quite clearly stealing that upperclassman's coat and wearing it as part of a wager."

"And Parkington saved your shanks. There was a tavern brawl, the coat got torn, somehow he ended by wearing it—"

"We were a trifle above oars," Buck admitted.

"Got caught by the upperclassman who then challenged him to a duel."

"Which dear Parkington won, of course. Fisticuffs, crude but effective. I would have chosen the épée."

"He never complained."

"He reveled in it. Actually thanked me later for the opportunity."

"I wish I hadn't been buried in books that night."

"Could have used your wrestling skills."

Cerestone smiled in remembrance. "We celebrated quite magnificently with your winnings."

Buck looked at the coach. "What a pity he has become so *horsey*. I should like him quite well otherwise."

What the viscount might have said in answer to this was lost in a tremendous blare of trumpets from across the river and the sudden reaction of the off-wheeler. The horse kicked out, jumped partially over its traces, squealed, and kicked the off-leader, which immediately tried to run away. Off went the postilion onto the grass; off went the coach flying driverless down the turnpike.

"Parkington!" both Buck and Cerestone shouted, looking at each other. They simultaneously broke into a run.

Meanwhile, the driver of the fourgon came awake, slapped the reins against the horses' withers, and off he went, racing, luggage and all, to catch the coach.

It wasn't long, however, before the coach came to a stop. The horses, not being experienced in driving, took the coach between two larches that stood far too close together and there the coach body stuck, front wheels torn off and spinning merrily down to the river. Henry emerged, stumbling against one of the larches. Showers of rose-red cones pelted his head. Cerestone and Buck reached him, helped him to another tree to sit down.

All three watched as the fourgon, the horses ignoring the driver, raced for the river. The driver sawed desperately on the reins then gave up and jumped. The horses swerved at the water's edge and everyone groaned as the wagon slowly, even gracefully, tipped over onto its side in the mud.

"The horses!" Henry exclaimed, trying to get to his feet.

"My supper!" Buck moaned.

The viscount turned to stare across the river, eyes alight. "The tourney!" he said with the hint of a smile. "It was a fourgon conclusion."

Chapter Two

Lady Alianora Maude Mathilda Cheney laid aside her psaltery and nodded as the knight graciously thanked her for her favor. He was Lord Savernake, a friend of her younger brother, Percy, and remarkably adept with the lance considering that this was his first venture into jousting. In the few days he had been at Grassmere he had proved gallant and charming but rather too interested in her. She had been forced to steal away to find some solitude among her willows.

She looked up at her father. He nodded with pleasure, his coronet wobbling a bit on his shoulder-length white hair. How much younger he looked today! His pale blue eyes sparkled, the brows like dove wings above them, and his beard, streaked with white and gray, was newly trimmed. He smiled broadly, a vast network of wrinkles spreading across his weathered face. She returned his smile, wishing that he could always be so alert and lucid, but knowing that after this evening his mind would slip away until the next tourney in the fall.

With a regal gesture, he signaled for the next joust to commence and she dutifully turned to watch. She enjoyed the tourney but never wished to be singled out as the queen of love and beauty—an honor bestowed on her yearly by her father since the age of five. And the day was only half done. Later this afternoon, the knights, fifteen of them from as far away as Northumberland, would choose sides and fight a brief battle called the melee. Someone was always wounded at this, although no one mortally as yet. She sighed. The worst was to come, however: the feast.

It would be a wondrous medieval feast whereat the cooks would vie with one another to surprise the earl; whereat the court musicians would announce each course with loud and often discordant flourishes; whereat streams of servants would compete to serve the lords and ladies; whereat a troupe of hired players would entertain the court with singing, dancing, juggling, and acrobatics; whereat she would again be required to sing and play.

She could not deny her love for song and dance, nor deny her love for the glittering world her father had created here at Old Grassmere. New Grassmere, a mere four centuries in age, lay farther away atop a long slope. Indeed, she knew little of modern life, although she had heard, certainly, something of the current world. It intrigued her, for she was full of a lively curiosity and brave as befitted an earl's daughter, but the unknown also frightened her.

"You are frowning, dear sister," whispered a voice in her ear.

It was her sister-in-law, Katie, married to her elder brother, William. Dancing brown eyes looked out from beneath a porkpie coif. Her brown hair was caught behind in a gold filet. "Truly, it is only one day," she continued, taking Alianora's hand and patting it.

"I know, Katie. I am afraid I have become too used to being alone here."

"It greatly pleases your father."

"Yes, and it is little enough. I should not begrudge

him an entire day of pleasure even if I must be the cynosure of all eyes."

Alianora stared out vacantly at the river. Katie looked at her, thinking how extraordinary it was that her dear sister-in-law was unaware of her unusual beauty and presence. It was a wonder to Alianora that so many knights paid court to her but no wonder to Katie. No one could ignore the porcelain skin, the gentian blue eyes, the long pale gilt hair bound now with colorful ribbons. She was graceful and filled with an inner calm that Katie envied, an envy that did not, however, affect her love.

Alianora's eyes focused suddenly. "Look, Katie! There are people watching us just across the river."

"I shouldn't be surprised! Imagine what a spectacle we present. Quite likely travelers on their way to London as we shall be in a scant three days."

Alianora sighed.

"Why, my dear, you will love London, especially during the Season," Katie said.

"To me, traveling to London seems like venturing beyond the edges of a map. There abide monsters." This was said with a smile, however.

"Perhaps there are a few, but I shall be with you. William has ordered me to be quite gay while he is away in the north and has allowed me unlimited pin money. Now you must agree he is not always so generous, and we must take advantage of him."

Alianora laughed, the sound like dancing grace notes. "You are quite right. William can be miserly."

"And I do understand your need for solitude. When we are in town, you need simply say that you wish to be alone. It was difficult for me to go among company again after—after—"

It was Alianora's turn to comfort her. Less than a year had passed since Katie lost her five-year-old son to a fever. She had not emerged from her chambers for three months after his death. London would be a marvelous distraction for her—Katie had always loved pretty clothes, dancing, and socializing.

"I shouldn't be afraid of a little change," Alianora told her. "I shall pretend to be a knight on a quest. Sir Gawain searching for the Green Knight or Galahad after the Holy Grail."

"And what shall your quest be?" asked Katie a little mischievously, recovering her composure.

"My quest?" Alianora looked surprised, then smiled to herself. "My quest. Perhaps to slay some dragons of Society."

Katie had one suggestion but declined to voice it. William thought it time that Alianora went out in society and found a husband, and he hoped that a Season in town would bring an acceptable offer. He would not push her into an unhappy marriage, but hoped for one as happy as his own.

A breeze brought the smell of river water and apple blossoms, a brief respite from the odor of sweating horses and oiled leather. Alianora clapped as her brother Percy again lowered his lance and charged at his opponent. William, finding such "play" beneath his dignity, was supervising the activity among the pavilions.

A great shout greeted Percy's fall and the winning knight presented himself to the earl, the countess, and the queen of love and beauty.

"Duty calls," Alianora said with a sigh and rose to meet the knight's request for a favor. To her relief, he asked only for her chaplet and not another song.

* * *

Ancient millefleur tapestries displaying scenes of great hunts, captured unicorns, and coronations covered the walls of the great banquet hall at Grassmere, ruffling with the passage of many people. It seemed the entire county had arrived to taste of the oxen roasted in pits outside, the pastries, the vast quantities of red mead. On a gallery built especially for the purpose a trio of musicians sat playing lustily, if not brilliantly, on their sackbuts whenever servants entered with another course, blowing ever louder as the noise of the crowd threatened to drown them out.

Alianora sipped mulled cider from a jeweled mazer, and smiled at her father, her mother, and her brothers William and Perceval who sat among the "knights" at a long trestle table perpendicular to theirs, as she struggled to ignore the terrible headache that throbbed behind her eyes.

The ferrier's wife, Mrs. Siphoner, at a distance from the salt, reared back and laughed like a barking mastiff; Mr. Barleycorn, the town alderman, stood up, waved his tankard of mead, and proceeded quite slowly and elegantly to fall over backward, elevated into unconsciousness; Mr. Malley, the local curate, jumped up on the table and danced among the bread-plates, dragging one of the townswomen up with him. This was all quite normal. This happened every year. And every year, the deafening noise, the heavy, smoky smells of food and bodies combined to strike like lead-weighted mallets on her head. Katie leaned forward and smiled sympathetically at her.

One after another marvelous creations appeared from the kitchens: a dragon flambé, not to be eaten but watched as the flames consumed the pastry to reveal a golden apple inside; a cockatrice made from the head of a rooster and bottom half of mutton; and a fountain that spouted wines from various sculptured terminals; followed by a garden of rose-bushes, all the branches gilt, all the flowers candied. All the food seemed to make her feel worse, although she tried heroically to taste of everything.

Around the branches of a gilded rosebush set in front of her, Alianora noticed that Perceval's friend, Lord Savernake, was once again staring at her. His dark eyes had fastened on her at the end of his joust when he had demanded the favor of a song. Even there in the open with her parents nearby she had felt uneasy beneath his gaze. Not that he had been anything but kind and courteous. Perhaps it was his face—his nose, thin and hooked, the dark, piercing eyes—and the way he loomed over her whenever they walked together, all reminded her of a falcon waiting on its prey. She could not say he had ever acted improperly, a lingering clasp when he kissed her hand, perhaps, or a hand too ready to grasp and guide her elbow even though she certainly knew her way about, but it could all be her imagination. She had been accused of allowing it to overwhelm her judgment at times.

Lord Savernake finally looked away from her to stare—she could almost say *glare*—at some newcomers at the banquet. She had heard that they were the victims of a carriage accident and met them only briefly before the feast. Her father had welcomed them, as he would welcome the world if it chose to come to dinner, and provided them with appropriate costumes. The three of them were sitting at ease, goblets of red mead in hand. She looked at them from behind the gilded rosebush and was surprised to find one of them looking back at her.

He was extraordinarily handsome—in a severe way. By the soft and flickering light of the candelabra, he looked as if a sculptor had chipped and carefully smoothed the cheekbones, the square jaw, the straight nose. Where his friends smiled and laughed, he seemed to take his pleasure quite seriously. He often rested his broad shoulders against the wall cushioned by tapestries and simply watched the scene before him as if it were a marvelous play. She felt he was a small area of quiet among so much noise, an oak standing still in a storm-thrashed wood. That quiet essence was more attractive to her than any of his physical attributes.

Far more attractive than Lord Savernake's everpresent smile and endless flattery. He was staring at her again and she looked down into her mazer, sniffing the clove and cinnamon in the cider, wishing that she could be away from this feast, beneath her favorite willow or riding across grassy fields to the river. And, perhaps with a companion. She'd never considered that before. A companion to share her quiet moments.

"Sweet *burde*," her father said, interrupting her thoughts. He gestured toward all the culinary wizardry before them. "I warrant you'll not see such wonders at court."

She looked up at him and smiled. "No, Father. Nothing half so wonderful." They had explained the London Season to him by telling him she was called to court to be one of the queen's maids of honor. There was some confusion as to which queen he believed to be in London, so only the title was used and he seemed well satisfied.

He then signaled for the chamberlain to announce the appearance of the final subtlety, which meant that all must turn over their plates and sing for their dessert by improvising a tune to the words baked onto the china. The musicians were mercifully silent, but the singing, as could be expected, resulted in a terrible cacophony. Alia hunched her shoulders, feeling the weight of the braids wound round her head. Her mother appeared behind her, moving from the other side of her father.

"Are you quite all right, Alia?" she whispered, seeing her daughter's normally creamy complexion pale.

Alia admitted to an aching head but was determined to remain. "Thank you for asking, Mama. I'll go straight to bed after I sing."

Lady Wynyate nodded, causing her thin, beaten-gold coronet to shift dangerously on her smooth brown hair. She smiled, adjusted the crown, and moved back to her elaborately carved chair.

Acrobats in red, green, and yellow jackets and tights leapt, somersaulted, and danced before them. Four footmen then entered staggering under the weight of a huge pastry, weaving to the left, to the right, always as if they were about to drop the dessert. The agitated steward directed them, until the pastry was set in one piece before the earl's table.

Well, almost one piece. It was a knight on a rearing horse facing a vicious-looking monster. The knight's lance was bent in the middle, hastily repaired with a thick slab of uncooked dough. The monster—it was not quite possible to discern exactly what species it represented—also reared with a large, fang-filled maw gaping menacingly, the lower jaw swinging by one hinge. As the crowd watched, a foreleg of the magnificent, muscled warhorse broke off and fell into the blades of pastry grass.

"Fortunes of war," drawled Lord Savernake and everyone laughed.

At the cry of "Whack off its head," the footmen gathered protectively before it. The monster's jaw finally fell with a crash and the banquet guests shouted in appreciative gusto. Lord Wynyate nodded and his chamberlain announced that it could now be eaten.

The guests jumped over the trencher boards and over each other to reach the concoction. Somewhere, hidden within, was a large gold ring, and everyone wanted that ring, which was supposed, according to tradition, to bring good luck throughout the year. At last, Mrs. Siphoner emerged dancing from the wreckage and holding the ring up high.

Finally servants cleared the mess. Alianora then presented a diamond brooch to the winner of the tourney, a Mr. Winton Dumphreys, a wealthy merchant with dreams of knighthood. He bowed over her hand then returned to his table. He had only just reached his bench when the servants began dismantling the trestle tables and carrying them away. The musicians came to life again, joined by tabors, pipes, and several more sackbuts, all adding more discord than concord but after so much mead had been consumed, no one really cared. They played several distantly recognizable measures of the *basse danse,* a French processional dance, and Lord Savernake was immediately before her, eyes alight and hand held out to lead her around the table.

Alianora joined him at the head of a line, facing the dais. They performed the reverence, facing each other but not directly. Savernake held her left hand shoulder high. He very gently rubbed his thumb over her palm.

"We have had too few opportunities to speak, my lady," he said, his voice as smooth as clotted cream.

"It is a pity, my lord," she said, arcing her palm away from the offending thumb. "Why at the events, I quite often find myself so busy that it is impossible not to offend someone. I trust that you have not found my father's hospitality less than generous."

"No, it is more than generous. It is the daughter's hospitality that has been lacking."

"Lacking, my lord?" she asked, raising her delicate eyebrows. The eyes beneath were cold.

"Missing. I would wish to see more of you, Lady Alianora," he said, drawing out her name as if it were a fishing line and she the fish. "I know that you prefer to ride early in the morning. Perhaps I could join you tomorrow."

"You could. I exercise my hawk at that time," she told him. "Quite early, in fact, it is often still dark when Stephen and I see to the birds." Stephen was her falconer.

"How exciting," he said with forced enthusiasm. "And how early. But to see you in the field, your beautiful hair in the sunlight, I should sacrifice all sleep."

They concentrated for a moment on the heel movements of the dance, heels out, then toe to toe, rise up, back down. The scent of sage and sweet woodruff rose up from the floor. Her father liked this man so she endeavored to be civil even while she longed to give him a final set-down. He presumed too much upon her goodwill.

"And I would be honored if you would allow me

to guide you about London when you arrive," he offered with what he considered a very friendly smile. To Alianora he looked more like a mastiff with its lips raised to protect a bone.

"I believe I shall be with my sister-in-law," she said, disguising her annoyance. She swayed outward then inward in a step called the *branle,* gracefully inclining her head. "I truly do not know our plans, my lord. It is difficult to commit myself at this juncture."

"London can be overwhelming on the first visit, especially to someone raised in the country."

"Yes, I imagine it might be but I shall not go unprotected."

"I have the entrée to many drawing rooms and it would be my pleasure to introduce you about." They turned about each other.

"You are more than generous, my lord."

And more than frustrated, he conceded as they made their final reverence, called a congé, and saluted the earl and countess. He led her to her chair then joined her brother Perceval on a bench. Some of the townspeople gathered together in a circle dance as the music started up once more.

"Your sister grows increasingly unfriendly, Percy," Lord Savernake commented, accepting a goblet from a passing page. He downed the contents. A footman leapt to refill it.

Percy, scowling as he grabbed the bottle of mead from the footman and drank directly from it, turned to look at his bench mate, fingers of pale hair very like his sister's falling into his eyes.

"She's not much for company, never has been," he said. "I don't blame her with this crowd."

Savernake looked surprised. "Are you not enjoying yourself? Perhaps not since you lost the final joust. I think it quaint, certainly eccentric. Not something I'd choose to do again, however."

"Crazy old geezer, makes everybody play a part whether they choose to or not."

"I found it amusing to play knight for a day. Surprised myself. I was quite good." He smiled to himself. "I believe your sister appreciated it."

"She likes anything that pleases m'father," Percy said, lolling back against the wall, cradling the bottle in his lap.

"That is how I will win her over, I believe," Savernake mused.

Percy sat forward, waving an unsteady finger. "Now, wait a minute. Nothing havey-cavey. Promised I'd introduce you—"

"Yes, indeed, and half your debts are forgotten as I promised."

"Didn't say I'd help you force her into anything. After all, my sister."

"I didn't say I'd force her into anything, my friend."

"No kidnapping." The finger insisted. Savernake shook his head, but Percy repeated, "No elopement."

"Ah, only if she specifically requests it, which she just might do." Savernake laughed softly. He looked at Alianora, sitting quite at ease beside her father behind the gilt rosebush. "She is unusually beautiful, a porcelain goddess," he continued. "Striking. That pale hair, her delicate features. She will be the rage of London whether she wishes it or not. Quite a novelty."

"She won't like it."

"No, indeed. But she does sing beautifully. That

will console me of an evening, particularly after a run of bad luck." He narrowed his eyes. "She will find London a frightening place after living here all her life and I will simply be there to comfort her."

"Just so she *wants* you to do that," her brother said vehemently.

"Just so." Savernake looked at him. "Relax, dear brother—in arms, that is. Your sister will be safe with me."

Percy rubbed his bloodshot eyes. "I'll pay you back, Savernake, no matter how long it takes. Don't need m'sister as payment."

"I have been unusually generous in waiting this long," his companion told him. "And you continue to run up debts so I must take my payment where I can.

"It's an addiction," Savernake went on. "Addiction to the thrill of the game, the excitement of the unknown." His eyes lit up at the thought. "The turn of the card, the click of the dice . . ."

"It's a curse."

"You grow redundant, my friend, and that is boring. You enjoy the play as much as any man."

Percy mumbled something incoherent. Savernake looked away, an expression of utter ennui on his face. He started to say something then frowned as he noticed another partner soliciting Alianora for a dance. Peter Everhurst. They'd once had a brief, nasty encounter over the viscount's sister, but Savernake, being reasonable and never one to come to blows, had backed away, letting a sneer be his final response. He had no trouble attracting heiresses, merely keeping them, and he expected that one day his luck would change. No gambler ever lost all the time. Except, perhaps, Perceval. He watched the viscount and Alianora thinking he had better move quickly to protect his interest there. It was entirely too bad that Cerestone's coach had broken down just across the Medway.

The musicians played the introduction to the final dance, an *estampie*. Alianora had just taken another sip of cider when over the rim of her mazer she saw someone approaching the dais. She almost dropped her cup; her headache fled.

He stood before her in a knee-length belted tunic, the two front panels of contrasting colors: one of red brocade, the other of black and white horizontally striped linen. Lord Cerestone waited patiently. By all rights, if she chose to dance, it should be with Lord Savernake once again, he being of higher rank, but her father had the power to dispense with that rule.

Lord Savernake did start to his feet but plopped down again when Lord Wynyate waved his permission to the viscount. Savernake grumbled then scowled as Percy laughed until he hiccuped.

Alianora took his hand, letting Lord Cerestone lead her to the center of the long room. His hand felt warm and comforting without the overly familiar thumb movements and squeezings of Lord Savernake. Lord Cerestone executed the small steps of the dance with only a few errors, creating new steps when he faltered.

"I have practiced this dance most diligently since teatime," he told her ruefully.

She smiled. "You have it almost perfectly, my lord."

Candlelight picked out the sparkle in his green eyes, the sheen of his dark hair, the softened expression as he gazed down at her. His mouth quirked as he saw the hint of mischief in her eyes.

"Yes, perhaps more stamping then *estampie*," he admitted.

"You've made quite an impression—" she began to say then bit her lip. Perhaps he would not appreciate her sense of humor.

"—on your toes," he finished for her and she joined him in laughter. "I am terribly rusty having spent my life between the pages of a book."

"It must be a book of large proportions."

He looked delighted rather than offended by her humor. "A tome of great caliber."

"Ah, then, you are a canon."

He laughed. "I serve as a rule."

"The Golden Rule, I may hope."

"Perhaps a bit tarnished. I shall polish all my skills in London during the Season."

"You travel to London?" she asked softly.

"As soon as our carriage is repaired."

"We too shall be leaving for London, in three days' time."

"How nice," he observed with a smile. "Perhaps we shall see one another again."

She hoped so then wondered at herself. She had never before felt so breathless around a man. Ordinarily, the knights swarming about her during the tourney completely put her off. She resented the intrusion on her privacy. Lord Cerestone, however, teased rather than flattered and held her hand as if it were a delicate flower. He did not treat her as if she were a creature to be charmed into obeyance but as a companion in the dance, equal to his moves.

Cerestone returned to his friends in a thoughtful

mood as the music changed, signaling that it was time for another couple to dance. Henry struggled to see him through his red-mead haze.

"Smitten," he decided.

Buck raised a gold-handled quizzing glass shaped like a whistle, which indeed it was, and studied the viscount.

"I believe you may be correct, dear boy. This is not auspicious."

" 'Spicious," Henry agreed.

Cerestone looked at one and then the other. "I find her attractive, yes, but it does not go beyond that."

"Top over tail," Henry warned.

"Ridiculous," the viscount said absently as he watched what was happening on the dais.

The earl, Alianora's father, spoke to his chamberlain. The chamberlain walked to the front of the dais and the loud music finally faded. He announced the next—and last—entertainment, which was to be Lady Alianora.

She unwrapped the psaltery from its velvet cocoon, set it on her lap, and began tuning the strings. Her headache was gone. That brief interlude with Lord Cerestone had lifted her out of this oppressive atmosphere. The psaltery was a small instrument, no more than a foot high, with a shallow sound box made of boxwood. The heat of the banquet hall had already altered the pitch of some of the strings, so she worked with them a moment. The crowd quieted down, anticipating the annual treat that would mark the end of another St. George's Day.

Once lost in the glory of the ballad, she forgot the listening ears. She sang about an elfin knight captured by fairies, returned to human life by the fierce love of his bride. Her voice touched each note like a carillon of crystal bells. The story became as real as their tournament and Mrs. Siphoner led the happy sobbing at the end.

Alianora, her eyes glowing, looked up to see Lord Cerestone looking back. Their eyes met and the world about them seemed to vanish.

Lord Savernake was not happy to see this. He wished for a giant cheval glass so that Cerestone's gaze might fall back on itself and turn him to stone.

Chapter Three

"Well, it's time I was off," William Cheney announced as he strode into the morning room. He was already dressed in a three-caped greatcoat with a flat-crowned hat, and he carried a leather crop.

The countess looked up from her coffee and plate of muffins. Even at this early hour she was cool and elegant, chestnut hair smoothly drawn back into a knot.

"We have been waiting," she said, nodding toward Katie who stood at the french windows clutching the pale blue brocade curtains. The early morning fog had lifted and the sun shone in pale mote-filled streams on her sad face, her lilac morning gown, and across the parquet floor. She swallowed then took a deep breath.

"I wish that you did not have to leave," she said, turning around, her voice a little shaky.

"I should be in Yorkshire no more than two months, I believe," he told her, joining her by the window and taking her hand. "You'll be quite distracted in London. You'll have your cousin Sarah for company, and you'll be doing me a great favor by bringing Alia out of the past, perhaps discovering a husband for her along the way."

Her smile was firm now. "Yes, I shall enjoy that. I always did love to attend parties."

"That's my girl," he said. "And perhaps, an entire new wardrobe to cheer you up."

"Well, perhaps," she said, looking into his hazel eyes.

William, so different in appearance from his younger siblings, Alianora and Percy, that they playfully accused him of being a changling, was dark where they were fair, was stocky where they were slender, was studious and practical where they were—well, Alianora was unworldly, Percy impatient with either world. Kissing his wife's hand, he led her back to the small breakfast table and she sat down.

"You will be all right while I am gone?" he asked his mother.

"Yes, I believe so," Lady Wynyate answered, setting down the delicate china cup. "Should your father wander off, as he does more frequently now, I'll have Segrave gather a party to look for him." She smiled, her smooth skin showing only a hint of age about the eyes. "We shall manage in one way or another until you return, my dear. I do hope you are able to enjoy your time away. We shall all miss you, of course."

"You may send word through Brunson if I am needed."

"I am more particularly worried about Percy," she said.

"The painting of the statuary was a mere lark, Mama. Being sent down from Oxford is quite a distinction among his set."

"You were never sent down," Katie pointed out.

"No, but then I was a stick."

"William!" His mother laughed. "There is nothing wrong with being a 'stick.' "

"I particularly love sticks," Katie added.

The bracket clock on the mantel began chiming and everyone fell silent until it had counted to ten.

Lady Wynyate raised worried eyes to her elder son. "I do wonder about the company Percy keeps."

William could not tell her the true nature of Lord Savernake so he said only, "Lord Savernake is not perhaps the best ton, but he is accepted everywhere."

"Well, if you do not think he is leading Percy astray then I shall not worry so much."

William did think the dissolute earl was leading Percy astray and planned to separate the two when he returned. Nothing too terrible could happen in two months, he believed. Percy had only a minimal allowance to gamble away. He glanced toward the windows and saw Alianora and the earl returning from their morning ride.

"I see Alia and Father are back. I did not think I'd have time to say good-bye." He leaned down and kissed his mother. "Good-bye, Mama. I'll be going now."

"Farewell, my dear. We shall do perfectly while you are gone."

He nodded. "Come Katie. See me off."

Alianora and Lord Wynyate rode up from the river at a gentle trot. Earlier they had crossed the peninsula and ridden around the castle ruins examining the damage done from festivities of the day before. Workmen were already busy striking the loges and taking up the fences and pavilions. To some it would seem sad to see the dream be dismantled, but Alianora was thankful only that it was over. Her father had wandered among the ruins, dressed in an embroidered brown tunic, dark hose, and boots, and a warm wool cape that lifted with the cool breeze off the river. He had even, at one point, begun to sing to himself and she joined in, being rewarded with a pleased smile.

She stopped not far from the house and watched as her father rode toward the stables. He saluted her, face flushed, almost youthful, his long white hair flapping beneath his plumed hat. She turned her old plowhorse around, walking slowly past New Grassmere on her way to the mews. It was time to exercise her hawk.

But she looked at the manor, face filled with yearning, as if to memorize every crack in the gray stone, every mullioned window, every sharp dip of the roof, every vine of the leafless ivy that would soon bloom and shade the walls again. She looked down at the beds of daffodils, the knots of primroses, pink, purple, and white, the kitchen garden, the orchard that walked over the hills into the distance, the trellised rose garden, her favorite willows. The lovely smell of spring in Kent, along the Medway, on Wynyate lands . . .

"No," she told herself. "I am not leaving forever. Only three months in London. Which is forever." She sighed then shook away the depressing thoughts as she reached the mews.

The mews, housing nineteen birds, was several hundred feet from the stables so that neither the animals nor the birds could frighten one another.

Stephen, her falconer, emerged into the sunshine carrying her goshawk, Belisande, and a pair of gloves.

"All is well with your beauty, my lady," Stephen told her, reporting on the particulars of the casting, which was hard and dry, and the state of moult, which was just beginning.

Alianora pulled on her gloves then put her wrist behind the hawk's legs as Stephen held the bird up and Belisande stepped back onto the glove. She could feel the pressure of the talons, but the glove was double leather over wrist and thumb so there was no pain. The hawk itself was a slate blue with mottled belly, still quite young. It wore a hood, jesses attached to the legs, and a bell tied to the deck feather in the tail so that it might be found were it to fly too far. Stephen climbed up on his horse, smiled a gap-toothed smile as he tied the lure to his saddle. The lure, a leather bag with chicken wings attached, would, when swung around and around, bring the hawk back if Alianora's unusual call did not. A whipper-in joined them bringing the hunting spaniels, Bucca and Finn, to flush out the prey.

They had hardly left the small building when William waved at them from the direction of the stables. Alianora turned Geoffrey and rode to meet him.

"Alianora," William greeted as she reached him.

"I'll be going now. I just wanted to ask you to take care of Katie while you're in London."

Alianora smiled in puzzlement. "Certainly, William, that is why I am going."

He looked up at her, started to say something then caught himself. He knew his sister. If he told her that the true plan was to remove her from Grassmere so that she might become accustomed to the modern world and find a husband, she would balk. But if he made it seem that she was only to provide companionship for Katie, she would accept the move more readily.

"Well, then," he said, clutching his beaver hat as a gust threatened to doff it. "I'll join you as soon as may be."

She wrapped the reins around the pommel, confident that Geoffrey, who was more like a placid, moving sofa than a horse, would not take off, and extended her hand.

"Have a pleasant trip, dear brother," she said.

"And you, dear sister," he said.

Lord Cerestone rose early the next morning, grateful that the earl had invited the three of them to spend the night. He also accepted the offer of a morning ride when he heard that Lady Alianora was out with her hawk. Riding swiftly over a hill and through a stand of beeches, he caught up with the party just as she sent the bird from her fist. He watched it dash across the long field, clipping daisies, to where the dogs had startled a number of small birds out of a thicket. The hawk rose, stooped but missed, then rose again.

A very high-pitched series of notes tickled his ear —not a whistle but more a melodious scream. He stared at Alianora. She held up her hand, singing the hawk back to her.

The hawk flipped its tail as it turned and flew straight for her like a slate arrow. After flapping its wings a few times above her, it landed lightly on her wrist.

"Oh, Stephen," he heard her say. "She's never returned so quickly." That beautiful laugh. "What a pity that I must halt the training now."

She was magnificent, Cerestone thought, in her fig brown riding habit that flowed over the flanks of her horse. She wore a large, plumed, felt hat over a coronet of white gold braids. He gave no greeting, not wishing to disturb her work, and so stayed just at the edge of the beech woods, watching.

How could he explain to his friends the strange allure she had for him—as if she had stepped directly from the pages of *Le Morte d'Arthur.* She studied her hawk as it flew again, her face in profile. He admired the cool, alabaster color of her skin, the cheeks tinged peach by the wind, the small nose, the determined chin. Fragile and yet filled with strength, someone who could present a threat to a vulnerable heart which, of course, his was not.

His mount shifted position and startled him out of his study. Neither Buck nor Henry would be able to understand his interest—Buck had grudgingly allowed that she was attractive in a peculiar way and Henry still did not see the women for the horses. Familiar only with women in society, debutantes only interested in party dresses and routes, Cerestone had been convinced that there was not a woman alive who could share his love of history and the printed page—or understand it. He must marry one day; as the eldest son he had a duty to the family name, but the thought of living with a wife who would interrupt his research with her prattling, who would complain when he forgot to come to dinner or forgot to dress for a ball—he let no servant disturb him while working in the library—made him cringe.

Until now Fanny had been the only exception. His sharp features softened as he thought of his younger half sister. She who was confined to a wheelchair after a particularly vicious fever some years ago would often sit in the library for hours with him, entertaining herself with books or helping him inventory the Woodhurst collection. He often took her into the garden when the weather was fine and invented stories to amuse her. Sweet natured, intelligent, and quiet—why could he not discover a woman to match the excellent qualities in his little sister?

He glanced back in the direction of Grassmere. His thoughts were overly colored by last night's pageant. Perhaps he had better return to his friends, although Buck was still getting his beauty sleep, and Henry had ridden with Trench to the blacksmith's to see about the condition of the coach. He reminded himself that they were a trio sworn against all aspiring mamas with hopeful daughters; they had agreed to return from London unshackled.

He had only just decided to leave when Alianora turned and saw him. She smiled a little, hesitantly, then looked back at her hawk. In all good conscience, he could not now go back without at least greeting her. Cerestone kicked his mount forward.

Alianora spoke softly to Belisande, careful to hold her just below eye level as hawks found the human face frightening. At the sight of Lord Cerestone her heart began to beat faster; she found it difficult to breathe. She had managed to smile in greeting then turned away as he frowned. Was he angry?

"Good morning, my lady," he said, suddenly by her side.

She took a breath. "A fair morning, my lord," she answered with an impish smile.

"Ah yes." He nodded in understanding. "Your hawk missed its prey."

" 'Tis not unexpected," she told him softly. "She is beginning to molt and is not as hungry as she might be." It amazed her how the words simply ran off her tongue when she was around this man. His expression might be severe when he was not smiling, but one had only to look in his beautiful eyes, as she did now, to see the humor and kindness there.

"Will you fly her again?" he asked.

She shook her head. "Only if we come across a flock of chickens. She does love a chicken."

His eyes danced. "Are there many such flocks about?"

"Only the tenants'. And they are loath to have a hawk descend among the hens."

"Puts one off one's laying, I should imagine."

She smiled, looking down. "Yes. There are no eggs for a week."

The kennel worker came up with them bringing the spaniels and a freshly killed coney. This Stephen would feed to Belisande when they returned to the mews. Alianora turned Geoffrey back toward the house and Cerestone followed.

"What call did you use for the hawk?" he asked conversationally. "It was unusual."

She laughed softly, looking at Belisande. "My

own special call, my lord. One that cannot be used by another."

"You were singing," he said.

"Singing, in a manner of speaking," she said, laughing.

Cerestone chuckled. "Will you be bringing your hawk to London with you?"

"No. I could not force her to leave her territory. She's been here since she was an eyass."

"That, I presume, is a baby hawk."

"Just out of the egg, my lord."

"It will be difficult then, for you to leave *her,*" he said sympathetically.

"Yes," she said softly, that one word carrying with it the message that she was reluctant to leave everything here.

"You will return," he said just as softly.

She looked up then laughed at herself. "Of course, I will. This is my home." Nevertheless, she was thoughtful. Would she be as content here once having seen London and what it had to offer? Katie could speak of nothing but the wonders to be found there.

The viscount frowned in annoyance as he spotted Lord Savernake riding swiftly toward them on a showy hack. The earl greeted Alianora with a flourish that disturbed her hawk.

"My apologies, my lady," he said, "for missing your ride this morning. I fear my man did not awaken me at the correct hour." He remained smiling even as she murmured "good morning" and refused to look up, staring instead at the space between Geoffrey's ears. He looked over her head at Cerestone in surprise.

"Cerestone, I hadn't noticed you," he said coldly.

The viscount raised an eyebrow. "Oh. Savernake. Is that you?"

The earl merely sneered as he was suddenly forced to control his nervous hack. The spaniels were dancing and barking, picking up on its nervousness. The hawk flapped its wings, something that appeared to terrify the horse.

Alianora worked to soothe the bird, speaking softly, thinking that Belisande would have taken wing by now if she had not put the hood on, between the earl's broad gestures and his mount's noisy head-tossing. She looked at Lord Cerestone who was frowning across Geoffrey's gently nodding head. His eyes softened when he met her gaze.

"Savernake," he said, sitting at ease in his saddle. "Have you lost your famed skill?"

The earl almost sawed on the reins. "Hard mouth," he answered through clenched teeth. The horse danced sideways.

"I do believe, Lady Alianora, that Lord Savernake's mount finds your hawk an object of terror."

"That, my lord, is why the mews is hidden from the stables," she said quietly.

With reins pulled taut, Savernake brought his horse closer to Alianora.

"My lady, I would be honored if you would consent to drive with me this afternoon," he said with a charming smile.

"Is your driving as skilled, Savernake?" Cerestone asked, a guileless tone in his voice.

Smoldering black eyes glared at him. "You may trust me completely, my lady."

Alianora sighed. Perhaps it would be better simply to humor him while he was here. It certainly was becoming difficult to avoid him. Ride out with him in order to earn some time without his presence.

"Impossible," Cerestone said, interrupting her internal debate.

"Impossible?" Temper flared in the dark eyes. "I was speaking to the lady."

"And, since she is engaged to spend the afternoon with me, you are also speaking to me. The answer is no. We do not wish to go driving with you."

Savernake looked at Alianora. "Is this true, my lady?"

"It is what I desire," she answered, an impish smile tugging at the corners of her mouth.

"Perhaps this evening, then, we may take a stroll in the gardens?"

"Now, there you are also behind the times," Cerestone told him.

The earl jerked on the reins. *"Now,* dear sir, just what is meant by that?"

"I do believe I was speaking English."

"I do believe there is an offensive note in your voice."

"A-flat."

Alianora choked.

"You accuse me of being a flat?" Savernake's voice rose. He reared back, which caused the horse to rear, which caused the spaniels to bark crazily, which caused the hawk to shriek, which caused the horse to take off, foaming at the mouth.

"Oh, dear," Alianora said and finally gave way to laughter, the bell-like tones ringing clearly through the din.

They watched as the earl bounced and jounced across the field, only just turning the horse from the thorny copse, but in so doing swerved so sharply that he lost his grip, boots, knees, and hands, and flew sideways into a bush. The sounds he made after that were not polite.

"Stephen," Alianora began, gasping for breath. "Stephen, perhaps you should see to him." Stephen nodded and rode away. "He is, I'm afraid, a guest," she added.

The viscount acknowledged this. "I apologize for goading him before you, my lady."

"But you would gladly goad him beside me." She lifted her eyebrows, imitating his expression.

He had to laugh. "Preferably out of your presence —if we must come together at all. He and I are not bosom beaux."

She smiled then turned to the hawk once more. The ruffled slate feathers lay down one by one at her words.

"I did mean what I said about this afternoon," he told her then wondered why he was leading himself to the slaughter. He should be running, riding as fast as Savernake away from her, but he could not quench the overwhelming desire to see her again.

"And I meant what I said, my lord," she answered.

They passed through the beech woods, smelling the sharp scent of worts crushed under hoof, passing in and out of bright sun patches until emerging at the crest of a rise. Cerestone pulled up and Alianora joined him. They both looked at Grassmere, rising above flowering chestnuts, the scythed lawn rolling up to it like a smooth green carpet. The whipper-in took the dogs on ahead.

"What it must be like to live here," Cerestone sighed.

Alianora patted Geoffrey's neck. "Like any other place, I should imagine."

He looked at her for a long moment. *"Could* you imagine what it is like elsewhere?" he wondered, struck with the thought that London would be a rude surprise to her, with hawks like Savernake on every corner. He smiled inwardly. One might say she was quite adept at handling hawks, but human hawks were more dangerous.

"I am not afraid," she told him.

"Ah, London frightens *me.* I shall be glad to return to Woodhurst."

"Your home?"

"Yes. A gift from Charles II to Sir Sydney Cerestone for supporting him in France. We were also raised to a viscountcy." His eyes grew a little distant, his features relaxed. "Just now the orchards are blooming, the wind from the southwest smells of the sea—there are the flowers, red campion, yellow water lilies . . . And when it rains the smell of newly plowed earth. The maids will be airing out the library grown musty over the winter." He laughed to himself. "I hope they remember to close the windows before it rains again."

"Woodhurst sounds lovely. You are as comfortable there as I am at Grassmere."

"However, I must see that my sister, Georgina, has her Season in town."

"And I must help my sister, Katie, recover from her loss."

"Yes, I was quite sorry to hear about her little boy. The pain must be unimaginable."

"She is better."

"It will not be all bad, I believe, in the city," he told her. "There are parks, places to ride and picnic.

There will be the opera and theater. And parties, of course, endless parties. Tiresome, but then one may make of them what one will. Interesting or boring. I will be giving a ball for Georgina to make certain society takes note of her. I hope that you will be able to attend."

"Will that not depend on your sister?"

"Not at all. This will not be a party for her friends, but for her to be seen—an expensive announcement that she is on the Marriage Mart."

"Marriage Mart?"

He looked a little embarrassed. "I am afraid that is what a Season *is* for a young girl. Her chance to look about for a husband."

That shook her a little and she couldn't quite explain why. She was not going to London for a *Season;* she was going as a companion for Katie.

"I had not realized," she said quietly.

"It is not spoken of, not generally, simply understood," he told her, thinking how much he took for granted. Did she really have no knowledge of society?—it spurred him into quite a feeling of protectiveness, which he immediately tried to fight back.

Stephen came up with them and reported that Lord Savernake had injured only his pride and was even now returning to the house. They were distracted by a horseman riding toward them from the stables. Henry. Cerestone smiled. On foot he might appear awkward, even clumsy in his stockiness, but once mounted, Henry was a centaur. The viscount, with an apologetic glance at Alianora, rode to meet him.

"Fixed," Henry announced as they met.

"The axle, the wheels?" Cerestone asked.

"New axle, new hubs, new shafts."

"The fourgon?"

Henry shook his head. "Needs new wheels, the near side."

"Yes, I was afraid they had cracked too badly to fix."

Henry peered at his friend, who seemed distracted, then looked at Lady Alianora just descending from the crest of the hill. "May leave after nuncheon."

"So soon," Cerestone said softly.

"Best."

Peter looked at his friend then slowly nodded. Henry was right. If he remained here any longer . . .

"Yes, it is best to leave," he agreed. It was the strangeness of this place that was attracting him so to Lady Alianora. When they reached town, he was sure he would barely remember her.

He escorted Lady Alianora to the mews and then left. She watched him leave, wondering how he could be so sympathetic and yet so distant. Who could say? They had known each other less than a day, and yet he had already sent ripples through her serenity. Shaking her head, she concentrated instead on the goshawk, admiring her fierce beauty for the last time. Stephen stood on the ground beside Geoffrey, his gloved hand outstretched.

"It was a fine session, my lady," he said, smiling.

She lowered the hawk. "Yes, I shall truly miss it."
Belisande stepped back onto Stephen's hand and he took it into the building. He removed the hood and placed it on its perch, reaching into a game bag for the freshly killed rabbit to feed it. Alianora turned away.

Lord Savernake strode into the stable yard as she stopped Geoffrey by the mounting block and slid off his huge back. She patted the old horse, saying farewell with a long luxurious scratching behind the ears. A groom waited patiently until she was finished then led the horse away.

Catching the long, velvet skirt over her arm, she stepped down to the yard, coming immediately upon the earl, who walked with only the slightest of limps. She awaited him; her father had taught her that it was better to face a problem than avoid it.

"You . . . you are well?" she asked, forcing herself to be civil.

He grimaced. "It was not pleasant, but I have survived. An unfortunate choice of mounts, I fear." He laughed a little, harshly. "I would be pleased to escort you to the house."

She could see the terrace from where she stood. She brightened. "Oh, there is Percy." He disappeared inside.

"He is more than likely hunting for your father," Savernake told her.

She looked down and sighed. She had overheard William upbraid poor Percy behind the library doors in a voice loud enough to carry to the second story. What her father could do for her younger brother she had no idea. William oversaw all the estate business now.

The appearance of the head gardener's children interrupted them and saved her from a walk with the earl. They had a large, brindled dog with them. It saw Alianora and stood up, putting its big paws on her shoulders, licking her face. She laughed, buried her nose in his coat.

"I shall miss you, Apollo," she told the dog, then gently pushed the animal from her. She looked at the children. "Davey, Molly, how are you this morning?"

"We're right fine, m'lady," said the boy most politely. His eyes, however, were wide with excitement. "Oh, m'lady, you must come see. You must."

His sister, two years his junior, nodded so vigorously that her dark curls bounced around her pinafore.

Alianora smiled, hardly noticing the dance the earl was performing in order to avoid Apollo's affections. "What is it, Davey? Something good?"

"Our rose, m'lady. Our rose has opened. Please, please come see. Da says you must look on't 'fore the dew is gone."

"Our rose has bloomed," she said thoughtfully. "How lovely! The first spring rose."

"Da'll set it in the garden today, if it comes warm enough."

"He's in the succession house now?"

Molly and Davey nodded. She held out a hand to each of them.

"Then let us have a look at our rose. Excuse me, my lord." She hardly glanced in his direction. Apollo ran after them.

"Tell us the rose story, m'lady. Molly wants to hear it." Davey's voice trailed away as they walked across the lawn.

"Well, there once was a lovely young lady named Beauty . . ." Of course, Alianora's version of *The Romaunt of the Rose* differed a good deal from Chaucer's, but he was not around to be scandalized.

The earl stood for a moment, staring in a most

ungenteel manner—one might even call the stare
vulgar—after the trio, mouth slightly agape. A look
of puzzlement then amazement then annoyance
crossed his face, then he straightened his torn jacket
and walked stiffly up to the manor.

Chapter Four

When they arrived in London, Henry dropped
Cerestone off at his home in Grosvenor Square and
he and Buck continued on to the Albany, where the
two of them would share Buck's rooms. The viscount stared up at the gray stone facade of Hurst
House as he stepped down from the carriage. It had
been five years since he'd last visited here and then
only briefly, to see that all was secured after his
father's death. He walked up the few steps and the
door swung inward.

"Beeley," he greeted.

"Welcome, my lord. We was wondering when
you'd arrive, precisely," said Beeley, taking the viscount's hat and coat.

"Ah yes, we did stop along the way."

"As we expected you should, my lord, knowing
your interests."

"We did have some difficulty with the coach. No
one was hurt, however," he added.

Beeley, Mrs. Chumdale, the housekeeper, and
several maidservants had come up from Woodhurst
to ready the town house for spring.

"Mrs. Chumdale has a light supper prepared, my lord; if you'd prefer, it could be served in the library."

Cerestone's eyes lit. "Why, yes. The library to be sure."

"I'll just inform Mrs. Chumdale." He left, handing the viscount's things to a footman.

Cerestone walked past the Yellow Saloon, the stairway, past a large, old, long-case clock that ticked quietly, and into the library at the back of the house.

It was a dark room with the deep sheen of mahogany paneling. Someone had tied back the maroon velvet curtains and the evening sun splayed across the plum, blue, and gold Turkish carpet, hardly adding one candle's worth of light. Peter walked slowly around, glancing over the shelves of books that reached to the ceiling, enjoying the slightly musty, leathery odor. He should have had these books transferred to Woodhurst and combined with those he was working on.

Beeley entered with a loaded tray and set it on a carved, heavy desk.

"Madeira, my lord, with supper. Tawny, as you prefer."

"Thank you, Beeley," Cerestone said as he completed his circuit, stopping before the hearth in which burned a lively, crackling fire.

"All is in order here, my lord," Beeley informed him. "Holland covers removed, linen aired."

The viscount pointed at the ceiling, lifting his eyebrows. Above the library could be found the drawing room. "Sideboards well stocked?"

Beeley bowed slightly, a twinkle in his brown eyes. "With my lady's favorite sherry."

"Good man."

Beeley then carefully lit a branch of candles and set it on the desk. "Shall you require anything else, my lord?"

The viscount moved to study another shelf of books. "No, not tonight. I believe I shall retire early. It's been quite a long day."

Beeley bowed and left the library, pulling the door shut behind him.

Choosing a book on the history of the Edwards, Peter carried it to the desk and sat down, staring at the Moroccan red leather binding, the gold foil stamping. The Edwards. Why choose this particular book? He knew why.

Laying the book aside, he started on the roast beef, attempted the parsley potatoes, struggled through the deviled kidneys, finally pushing the plate away, appetite deserting him. He stood up and moved around the desk to a comfortable, over-stuffed chair by the fireplace, carrying the Madeira decanter with him.

For a while he savored the wine while anticipating visits to booksellers, to museums, to any number of literary salons, but little by little thoughts of a girl dressed as a medieval maiden intruded—how the Madeira, when held up to the firelight, was as pale and golden as her hair. He lowered his glass. What foolishness! He was no romantic. He was practical, sensible, and he was quite happy with his books and his friends. He did not need anyone else in his life.

With that decided, he proceeded to empty the decanter. Eyes drooping, he found himself imagining Lady Alianora—Alianora, saying her name aloud to himself—sitting in this very library, gracefully plucking at her psaltery, singing a soft ballad as he read by the fire.

No, he thought, as he fell asleep in the chair. What a farrago of romantic nonsense . . . He was a historian not a Gothic novelist.

He awoke early the next morning when a maid carrying a coal bucket tripped over his outstretched legs. She apologized profusely, miserably, and he assured her it was entirely his fault. Saying that he would leave her to her work, Cerestone walked up the stairway to his own undisturbed bed.

His mouth felt as if he had stuffed it with cotton, his head felt swollen, his neck objected to any attempt at straightening. There were times when he wished his servants weren't so compulsively thoughtful. One punch to the shoulder, one kick in the shins and he would have gladly sought his bed. Trench would have had no such reservations, but he had remained behind to supervise the fourgon's repair.

He should not have enjoyed the Madeira quite so much. Undressing, he pulled back the covers, and fell onto the cool linen sheets.

He slept until the afternoon when Trench entered the room with a loud "Lovely day, my lord," and proceeded to expose the room to sunlight.

Cerestone cringed then realized he felt better; even his neck was rather more flexible now. He sat up, sniffing.

"Coffee, Trench," he said in a hoarse voice.

"Jamaican, my lord, with just that touch of rum and vanilla." Trench lifted the silver urn steaming on a side table and poured the coffee into a china cup decorated with tiny blue flowers. He presented it to the viscount.

"Ah, a rum touch, and it's fresh," Peter sighed after sipping it.

"I stopped at Garroway's upon arriving, my lord. They had a ship newly arrived with a hold full of the beans."

"What luck." He finished the cup and held it out for more. Trench obliged then continued laying out the viscount's clothes for the afternoon. Cerestone began to feel much better, quite human, in fact.

"Trench, I'm to meet Mr. Rasherly and Mr. Parkington at Hatchard's this afternoon."

"A little preliminary browsing, my lord?"

"Yes." He sighed at the unspoken request. "Is there perhaps a particular book you might possibly be interested in purchasing?"

"As a matter of fact, my lord—" Trench named five novels recently out of the Minerva Press.

"Trench," Cerestone asked between sips. "What is so terribly interesting about evil sultans, haunted castles, and fainting heroines?"

Trench drew up his stout chest indignantly. "There is far more to the stories than what you have suggested, Master Petey. For those of us who appreciate it there is fear, excitement, and, in particular, a good moral ending."

The viscount winced at the childish nickname. Trench used "Master Petey" only in private, he granted, in particular when he wished to be condescending.

He was far too tolerant, Cerestone realized. But what was one to do with someone who had put him on his first horse? Who had wiped away a small boy's lonely tears? Laid out his first pair of long pants?

"I suppose your value as a valet greatly masks your eccentricities," he allowed generously.

"A compliment, my lord. And so soon upon arising."

Cerestone choked. "What a complete hand you are, Trench."

"Yes, my lord."

"Have all the trunks arrived?" he asked after a moment.

"Some a little battered and water stained, otherwise intact, my lord." Trench cocked his head, touched his pocket. "Oh yes, several missives arrived while you was asleep. One, I believe, from Lady Finsbury, another from her daughter, Miss Cressida."

"Aunt Sophia," the viscount said as if the name were bitters dropped into his cup. "I might have realized she would be watching."

Lady Finsbury was the sister of his stepmother, a woman possessed of a loud, unpleasing voice and pushy personality, who lived just across the square. For some time now she had been throwing her daughter Cressida his way. And Cressida, a duplicate of her mother, being only the tiniest bit more clever, was nothing loath to this idea. Peter remembered the presence of his friends with particular gratitude.

"Throw them in the fire," Cerestone ordered hopefully.

"My lord!"

"Oh, all right, Trench. I'll read them after breakfast."

A little more than half an hour later he was at

table, enjoying the *Morning Post.* He was dressed in a comfortable coat of bottle green kerseymere and buff breeches, cravat rather simply and loosely tied, hair combed into shining waves. He ate absently, spreading the newspaper out on the table before him. Before he could turn to the fourth page, he was interrupted by Beeley who stood at the door, clearing his throat in an urgent manner.

The viscount looked up. "What is it?" He did not like to be disturbed at breakfast, even if he was taking breakfast at teatime.

"They have arrived, my lord," the butler announced.

"They? They who?"

"Lady Cerestone and her—entourage."

The viscount jumped up immediately, walked to the window and looked out on the square.

"You mean 'cavalcade,' Beeley. Good God, what a mass of luggage. How many carriages are there?" He counted. "Four. It appears as if we're setting up a blockade out there." Cerestone frowned. "Were they to arrive today? I had it in my mind for next week."

Beeley looked a little regretful. "This was to be the day, my lord, precisely. Only we imagined they would arrive in the evening."

"Yes, a pity," the viscount mumbled grumpily. "I must send an excuse to my friends. Beeley, stay a moment." He walked to the drawing room, dashed off a note, and handed it to the butler. For now, he must delay his pleasure. He then went down the stairs.

The dowager viscountess was just descending from the carriage with the help of a footman. She was dressed, or one might say more precisely, was *draped* in a cloud of celestial blue dimity generously flounced and a traveling cape of deep blue wool. A bonnet of fawn twilled sarcenet decorated with ribbon rosettes covered her dark curls. In her hands she carried a parasol of fawn silk with a fringed awning and a net reticule heavy with medicinal bottles. She looked up at her stepson with tragic eyes.

"What a trial, my dear," she said softly, faintly. "These dear children have driven me to distraction. I simply must have a long rest. You do not mind that we descend en masse this way?"

What could he say? He kissed her upheld cheek. "No, Mama. You were expected."

"Good. Now, my dear, will you see that everyone is settled? I will just speak to Mrs. Chumdale to apprise her of our needs and then will rest at last. However, Peter, I must speak to you before you leave for one of your clubs. And, of course, you will see that a doctor is engaged for Fanny."

"Yes, of course. Is she not improving?"

"Not as one would wish. I believe she has missed you, but then one can never tell with that child. Such a reticent mind. Not as sociable as our dear Georgy. Or Georgina as she prefers now."

His mouth tightened. "I'll try to keep that in mind."

With an airy wave that sent clouds of otto of roses his way, she turned and gracefully ascended the steps.

The viscount moved to the door of the carriage, ordering the footman to help with the luggage, but stepped back quickly when a little bundle of energy exploded from the vehicle.

"Bobbin!" Cerestone called as his six-year-old

half brother, Robert, ran into the house. The small boy returned to the door.

"Peter! We are here at last!"

"So one may observe. I could wish a little less haste, however."

"We have Hector with us. May we leave for the park soon? Mama says there is a park Hector may run in."

"Later, youngling. For now, go on in and look around the house," he offered. "Touch nothing as yet. I will show you what you may play with. Understood?"

The boy nodded, his face the good-natured image of the late viscount. The viscount turned to hand out his eldest half sibling, Georgina. She greeted him coolly, neither smiling nor frowning. Her clothes reflected her mother's taste, light, frilly. Georgina, unfortunately, had inherited her grandmother's looks, a face that was broad, a nose a shade too long, but style and demeanor, as well as her generous portion, would make her a success.

"Georgina, you are looking extremely well," he observed.

"I have been quite happy away from Woodhurst," she replied. Meaning, of course, that she was quite happy wherever he was not. She had still not forgiven him for the Savernake episode.

"We should have a talk very soon," he told her.

"If you mean to be horrid and tell me what I cannot do, I won't listen," she warned him in a voice that moved from cool sophistication to childish petulance.

"You are still quite young, Georgina."

"I am quite old enough."

"Yes, and that is the problem," he said, shaking his head as she flounced into the house.

Cerestone then climbed into the carriage and sat down beside his youngest sister.

"Well, Fannikins, at long last I have you again."

"Oh, Peter," she said, smiling in a remarkably mature and friendly fashion for a ten-year-old. Although it was not cold, she was swathed in shawls, a small, pale face amid the cashmere.

"Mama tells me you have not recovered as you should from your Christmas illness."

"I am well enough," she said bravely.

"I think you did not enjoy your cousins."

She shook her head slowly, wispy strands of light brown hair escaping the shawl.

"Did you miss me?" he asked, then smiled as she nodded vigorously. "Well, we shall have to rectify that. Come, I'll carry you into the house." He gathered her into his arms and maneuvered carefully out onto the pavement.

"You'll have your own room overlooking the garden, with lots of sunshine. And tomorrow, perhaps Miss Tavisser could take you to the park. The sun will put some color into your cheeks."

"But, Peter, *ladies* never seek the sunlight. It makes for freckles." She giggled a little.

"Yes, I can just hear Georgy saying such a thing." He stepped up into the foyer, paused at the bottom of the stairs, then started up to the first story. "But you have no freckles," he objected. "You have skin of pure alabaster." Alabaster. The word distracted him for a moment as a vision of Alianora's pale skin came to mind. He concentrated instead on where he put his feet. "Quite the thing, actually," he continued.

He set her down on the bed when they reached her room. The soft cotton coverlet was embroidered with daisies to match those on the bed hangings and curtains. Two dolls in muslin gowns sat comfortably together in a small rocker. Fanny noticed them immediately.

"I bought them for you while you were away," he said, bringing them to her. He looked at the door frowning. "Where is Miss Tavisser?"

"Oh," Fanny replied, laying aside several of her shawls and putting the dolls, one with gold hair and one with dark curls, on the pillow beside her. "She takes most dreadfully ill whenever we travel. Mama switched places with her this time and rode with us."

"She must still be out there. It appears I must put you to bed myself."

"Must I?" she asked wistfully. "I do wish to see the house."

"As soon as you have rested, a complete tour, on my honor as a bookworm."

She giggled, but the giggle turned to a cough. Cerestone sat down, pulled her into his lap and held her, stroking her hair until the spasm abated.

"Now, in the future, you must not laugh," he ordered sternly.

She smiled weakly. "I'll try not to."

"And I'll endeavor not to be so very funny."

Calling a maid to prepare his sister for a nap, Cerestone left to find Bobbin. After settling his little brother in the nursery and admonishing him to await the arrival of his governess before leaving, the viscount returned to tuck Fanny into bed, careful to include the new dolls.

"Peter!" she cried as he turned to leave.

"What is it?" he asked in concern.

"I cannot sleep unless you tell me a story."

"Ah," he said, recognizing the ploy. Nevertheless, he sat down on the bed, smoothing the hair from her face. "I just happen to have an amazing tale to tell you. It occurred on the road to London, only the day before yesterday, in fact." Somehow, it already seemed a long time ago.

"What is it, Peter?" she asked breathlessly, her eyes a little brighter in her illness.

"This is a true story," he began in a voice deliberately filled with wonder. "Although you who live in the present world may find it difficult to believe, I saw an enchanted castle on an island in a river, arising from the mist as we rode over a hill. At first there were trumpets, loud and haunting, rolling across the water . . ."

He continued, drawing out the descriptions the way she loved him to do. In truth, he could do justice to any of Trench's novels, but he would never have admitted it. He became especially poetic when he spoke of Lady Alianora. Alianora, the medieval princess with gossamer gold hair as if the pale dawn light came to rest on her head. Fanny clasped her hands together at this part, eyes wide with interest. But in little time, her eyelids drooped, not a comment on his storytelling but on her own weakness. Cerestone lowered his voice, letting it fade as her eyes closed. Very gently he stood up, gazing with a frown at her pinched face, and quietly left the room.

The remaining part of the afternoon was quite busy. After enjoining Beeley to find a very good doctor, and seeing that all the trunks, bandboxes, and portmanteaux, and the tottering Miss Tavisser, were safely bestowed at last, Cerestone returned to his newspaper. But Bobbin, who seemed to possess a supernatural amount of energy even for a small boy, asked if the viscount could now take them to the park as Hector was quite anxious for a run. Hector, as if to prove these words, bounded into the breakfast room, a woofing mountain of a dog, who circled the breakfast table three times then came to rest with his bristly head on Cerestone's lap.

He looked at Bobbin who smiled confidently. "Hector says we should go now."

"Hector is quite eloquent," he commented and rose.

And off they went, cutting across Grosvenor Square down to Piccadilly and thence to the park. Hector flew over the new spring grass and disappeared for some time. Fortunately, the dog was not the slightest bit interested in cattle so the cows were left undisturbed. Ah, but waterfowl! A gold mine, one might say, and Hector mined the ornamental ponds. He returned extremely wet and muddy.

Bobbin, meanwhile, trampled through flowers, ran at the cattle, climbed trees, and hugged Hector when the dog returned thereby thoroughly dirtying his nankeen suit. The viscount declared that they had all had enough exercise and hooked on Hector's lead once more, ordered that both of them be given a bath immediately upon returning.

At the door, Cerestone handed the animal to a footman, noting that the young man did not flinch at the thought of giving such an animal a thorough wash. He would keep him in mind for similar duty in the future. Bobbin he sent upstairs. Beeley caught him as he turned with relief toward the library.

"Lady Cerestone wishes to see you in the drawing room, my lord."

The viscount sighed, head down, hand on the stair rail.

"And I have managed to engage Sir William Blizard to have a look in on Miss Fanny, my lord. He is unable to leave the hospital this evening but will be here tomorrow by noon."

Cerestone looked up. "Yes, I have heard of him."

"And Mr. Rasherly and Mr. Parkington will meet with you at Watiers this evening."

The viscount nodded then walked slowly up to the drawing room. He took a deep breath and entered.

"Mama, you wished to see me," he said.

She sat in one of the gold and black striped satin-back chairs, elbow resting on a small table as she lifted a delicate glass of sherry to her lips. She seemed to disappear into the primrose ruffles of her robe de chambre.

"Yes. I intend to speak to you of Georgina."

The viscount glanced longingly at the sideboard but decided not to drink, thinking that later he would indulge at the club. He sat down in an armchair and waited patiently for Lady Cerestone to continue. After sipping her sherry once more, she spoke.

"Georgina must have some new gowns immediately. I have arranged for Madame Portoneaux to come here tomorrow." She eyed him as if she imagined he would object but Cerestone merely nodded. "She shall, of course, require a court dress, which is always quite dear."

"Within reason, Mama, certainly. Georgina does not need a thousand brilliants and pearls to weigh her down."

"One needs to sparkle a little, Peter."

His eyes danced. "Five hundred brilliants, then, but no more."

"You are teasing, of course. I know that you would wish your sister to appear well at the Drawing Room."

"Yes, I certainly would wish that."

She sighed, finishing her sherry. The viscount arose and refilled it for her. "It has been a difficult year. Georgina can be so—" She hunted for a delicate word.

"Stubborn?" Cerestone supplied.

"Precisely, although perhaps 'headstrong' is a better word. When she is at her tantrums, I find I must retire to my rooms or risk a megrim."

He had had a taste of his sister's temper. When he had carried her away from school last year he created a terrible scene, screaming that he was abducting her, that he was beating her, begging loudly for help from any passerby, be it a pedestrian or an entire stagecoach. He hoped that one day she would realize she had embarrassed herself far more than him.

"She will, most likely, be fine in society. A little town polish goes a long way."

"There is the matter of her marriage." She lifted her glass then lowered it. "I depend upon you, Peter, to introduce her to the proper sort of people."

"By proper, you mean, of course, 'eligible'?"

"Of course, my dear."

A mischievous light appeared in his green eyes. "Shall I consult my Debrett's then?" He ticked off a list on his fingers. "Would you care for a title with a long ancestry? Will a baron do or must it be a higher rank? I have not been in town for some time and find myself quite ignorant."

She smiled languidly. "You are teasing again, but I believe you understand."

"Certainly, Mama. Georgy will marry the proper sort, I promise."

Beeley interrupted them with a discreet cough.

"My lady, my lord, there are visitors below. Lady Finsbury and her daughters, Miss Finsbury and Miss Cressida."

Peter grimaced, remembering the notes he had neglected to read. Lady Cerestone bid the butler send them up.

Lady Finsbury sailed into the drawing room like a Roman galleon with two small boats in her wake. She was a large Junoesque woman, dressed all in rustling purple taffeta. Her younger daughter Cressida, a stylish, attractive young lady who knew her own worth, took the viscount's recently vacated chair. It was not the proper thing to do, of course. Young, unmarried ladies did not sit where a bachelor had just been sitting. Cressida knew this and she calmly defied anyone to mention it. No one did in the flurry of greeting and her gesture was wasted.

Cerestone kissed his aunt. The two dowagers touched cheeks and moved to a confidante. Jane Finsbury stood quietly. She was only a little older than Cressida, not nearly as pretty but possessed of kind eyes and a sincere smile. The viscount took her hand and squeezed it fondly.

"Refreshment, Beeley," Lady Cerestone ordered. "And send for Miss Georgina." She looked at her sister. "Sophia, it has been an age."

"Susan," Sophia said in her scratchy staccato voice. "We would have preferred your company at Christmas."

"I was obliged to attend upon Uncle Willowbury, as you recall."

"Has he included Robert in his will at last?"

"I believe so. He hinted as much—" They continued speaking.

Cerestone let go of Jane's hand and moved to a chair across from Cressida, remarking that she looked quite fetching.

She leaned forward and said softly, "You received my note, Peter?"

"Yes," he admitted. "I apologize—I've had no time to read it."

"Oh." She sat back, pouting, knowing that a pout showed her small, beautiful mouth to great advantage. "I had hoped that you would keep your promise."

"Promise?" he asked, puzzled.

"That you would teach me to drive, of course," she said as if he couldn't possibly forget such a treat. "And I thought tomorrow would be nice. In Hyde Park, naturally."

"In the park? That might be dangerous."

"No, it wouldn't, Peter. Why, everyone drives at such a slow pace that it couldn't possibly be the slightest bit dangerous."

He thought about it a moment. "I think that for your first lesson we should choose a time when the park is uncrowded. Late morning."

"But Peter," she started to object then thought better of it. She smiled. "Late morning is quite all right."

"Good. I'll come for you at ten," he told her without noticing that her eyes widened at what seemed to her an extremely early hour.

At that moment, Georgina arrived. She had a kiss for her aunt, and, with barely a civil glance at her brother, she carried Cressida off to her room. Cerestone joined Jane who had been sitting quietly on the window seat looking at a magazine she'd found on a table. She looked up and smiled.

He sat beside her. "Have you finished the book I lent you?"

She laughed. "If I hadn't finished it in a year I'd be a sorry reader, wouldn't I?"

"If you'd read anything at all in a decade you'd be unusual in the general populace."

"Now, Peter," she scolded. "Most people might have read a Gothic romance."

He narrowed his eyes.

"Yes, I see," she said with a chuckle. "You do not consider them 'books.' Don't be such a snob."

"Well." His glance lightened. "It does prove that both the author and the reader know their alphabet."

"Well, there, you see! They are quite useful after all."

He looked at her, the slight strain hidden behind her smile. "I thought you vowed never to come to London."

"I did vow. Strenuously. But no vow holds water with Mama if she disagrees. She must bring both her daughters to London for the Season."

"To detach one daughter from the local vicar?" he asked softly.

She looked down, blushing. "If you mean Andrew, then I do believe so."

"Of course I mean Andrew. Has he spoken yet?"

"Not in so many words, but we have an understanding." She glowed at the thought of him then looked at her cousin. "Have you found someone yet?"

Lord Cerestone's eyes grew distant. "No."

"Well," Miss Finsbury said, noting his look. "You have been quite isolated at Woodhurst. Perhaps there will be someone for you in London."

He shook his head.

"I would see you happy, dear cuz," she insisted.

He smiled. "I am happy. You know me, dear cuz —books, books, books. My life is full and interesting."

Now why did Miss Finsbury give leave to doubt that? Something in his tone of voice, the feeling that he held something back.

She was about to tease him further when a terrible commotion below interrupted them. They heard Bobbin yell "Hector!" and Cerestone knew immediately the cause of the problem. Georgina and Cressida came in from the landing, shrieking inelegantly, chased by a very wet and foamy creature.

"He's ruined my gown!" Cressida screamed in a voice remarkably like her mother's.

Georgina joined her behind a large sofa. "That wretched, wretched dog! Peter, do something!"

Struggling not to laugh, Cerestone went after the animal, but his hands slid right off the soapy coat.

To Hector, this was a game; tag was a favorite of his, and he leapt onto the confidante to escape. Unfortunately, he didn't notice until far too late that it was occupied by two ladies. They screamed and pounded him with their reticules.

Ah, thought Hector, a new game, this one called 'fetch,' wherein *he* trained the humans. He opened his cavernous mouth, snapped it shut on Lady Finsbury's reticule, and raced out the door. Lady Finsbury did not cooperate, being a remarkably untrainable human, fainting heavily instead. The viscount followed Hector down the stairway trying to appear stern and angry when he spotted Bobbin, but, in the end, leaned weakly against the railing, yielding at last to his mirth. He looked up to see Jane, only a little worse for wear, laughing with him.

Chapter Five

"The city air, how I have missed it!" Katie exclaimed as they pulled into Bruton Street just off Berkeley Square. Her dark eyes were alight, her face flushed.

Alianora wrinkled her nose as a footman opened the door and let down the steps. The air did not smell particularly good to her; in fact, it seemed heavy with soot from the coal fires and quite a nasty, lingering smell of garbage. Inside, their town butler Shoop informed Katie that a guest was already awaiting them. At that moment, the drawing room door flew open and out bundled a comfortable dumpling of a woman. Sarah Bowman, Katie's cousin, greeted Katie with a soft, surrounding hug, her huge ruffled cap waving in the cool breeze, the nice odor of lavender/linen wafting from her. She made mother-henlike cluckings as she turned and hugged Alianora, saying, "My other lamb!"

Alianora paused as the others went into the house, looking up and down Bruton Street. There were houses all shouldering one another, so close together, so close they almost shut out the sky. A gust of wind blew right through her thin traveling suit and pelisse and she shivered. These were Katie's clothes, borrowed until she and Katie could visit a London modiste. She did lament the short hem—why, her carriage slippers could be seen in their entirety and not a little of the ankle when she descended from the carriage! She shivered again. How she missed her velvets and heavy furred capes!

They had dinner that evening in the Blue Saloon where a cheerful fire crackled in the hearth. Here there were indeed blue needlework chairs, blue satin chinoiserie wallpaper, dark blue brocade curtains, Delft tiles surrounding the fireplace. There were portraits of ancestors all staring down at the long dinner table. Alianora was glad Katie had invited Mrs. Bowman to stay with them. She was full of gossip about the Fashionable World.

"Oh, Alianora!" Katie said as she sat at the head of the table. "You have no idea how much better I feel! Of course," she added, sobering for a moment, "I shall never completely recover but I must try, for William's sake. And he is depending on this visit to lift my spirits."

Alianora sipped from her small wineglass, as a

footman served her roast beef. Ah, beef, she sighed softly. "I am as empty as a tabor."

Katie laughed. Mrs. Bowman opened her liquid blue eyes very wide. Alianora paused, looked at them.

"Alia," Katie said with a smile. "A lady must never admit she is hungry, it is poor ton. We must appear to eat nothing."

"I cannot eat?" she asked, horrified, then she narrowed her eyes. "You're teasing. That cannot be one of the rules of society."

"Well, yes, it is," Katie admitted. "However, the rule is that we never admit we're hungry and we eat almost nothing in public."

"Then it is all right for me to eat dinner here, now?" Alianora asked with a half smile.

"Oh yes, but not when we are dining elsewhere, specifically not at a supper ball."

"Not at a supper ball?"

"Perhaps it is a bit contradictory; society's rules are rarely logical," she said ruefully. "But they exist and must be obeyed or you risk censure."

Alianora frowned at her roast beef. "I don't know if I'll be able to remember them all."

Katie smiled sympathetically. "We'll help you, of course. And you are naturally quiet and polite, which is all that is truly required of a young girl."

"Is this to be my 'Season'?" Alianora asked hesitantly.

"Why, it might be, if you wish." Alianora did not wish but said nothing.

Mrs. Bowman waved her fork emphatically, endangering the portion of creamed asparagus thereon. "And beware of heathens. London is full of the creatures."

"Heathens?" Alianora asked, startled.

"Barbarians, vultures," Mrs. Bowman supplied.

"Vultures?" Alianora asked with a smile as she began to understand. "I am rather good at training hawks."

It was Mrs. Bowman's turn to appear startled. She knew nothing of falconry.

"Alianora and her father raise falcons and hawks," Katie explained.

Mrs. Bowman humphed. "Then, I might say lilies among the weeds."

"William will be here in June," Katie assured her.

"Yes. I shall be your bulwark until then. Just let a heathen cross this threshold!" She punctuated this fierce remark with a snap of her fork and a piece of asparagus flew past Alianora's ear. Alianora continued to eat calmly.

"Any heathen would be properly terrified, I am sure," Katie observed. "I do, however, intend to enjoy myself. Alia, what do you think of the city thus far? Is it not amazing after Grassmere?"

"Yes, it is amazing."

"You don't like it already. I can tell."

"Well, no, but I will try to like it while I'm here. I know there are parks." She let herself think briefly of Lord Cerestone. Was he already in the city? "I do like your house, especially the garden in the back. The rooms are beautifully furnished."

She smiled. "Well, perhaps, some things are a bit dated, but I shall not know what is new until I begin visiting again." She brightened. "And tomorrow, as early as possible, perhaps noon, we shall go to have new dresses made, and spend the time shopping for bonnets, slippers, and gloves, and so much more."

Just as Lord Cerestone had said—parties, so many parties. He hadn't mentioned the wardrobe she would need, but then a gentleman would not have.

"And we'll find you a nice young man," Mrs. Bowman said brightly, quailing a little when Katie immediately and emphatically shook her head at her. Mrs. Bowman's small eyes widened and she covered her mouth.

Alianora froze inside, slowly lowering her fork. Of course! She *was* here to find a husband—that was why William had ordered her to town with Katie, not just as a companion. She was to be put on the Marriage Mart, however unwillingly!

Katie searched for a topic to distract her. "You will be able to dance, quite frequently. There are so many balls, routs, ridottos, drums. You'll have so much fun! I know you love to dance."

Alianora heard her dimly and nodded.

"And Alia, I have already received the Lord Chamberlain's summons to the Drawing Room Thursday next so that you may begin your debut properly. As a matter of fact, that is the first thing we must do: have you fitted for a court dress. And we have vouchers for Almack's—my mama, when she was alive, was such a good friend of Emily Cowper's. There are already so many invitations that I shall spend the entire evening merely sorting through them."

Alianora hated to say anything to stem the bright flow of chatter so she remained silent. She well remembered the subdued Katie at Grassmere last spring but also recalled how she used to be: just this way, charming, anxious to see that all around her shared her joy. It was, no doubt, why the somber, stolid William had been so struck by her.

But marriage for her? What type of man would accept her and her odd family? And how could she leave Grassmere? The thought almost made her lose her appetite. Even Lord Cerestone—a man she found kind and attractive—even he would take her away from her home if she married him.

"—and I must bring in a dancing master, although, of course, you cannot waltz at any ball until one of the patronesses of Almack's has given you her permission. There is a new dance, introduced last year called the quadrille de contredanse that even I must be taught. So we may learn together."

Alianora took a deep breath. "Yes. I would like to learn. Katie, I am a little tired—"

Katie was immediately all sympathy. "Of course, my love. It all is quite too much, isn't it?"

Alianora nodded, holding back her tears.

"Of course, my little lamb," Mrs. Bowman added. "You must both be exhausted."

Katie looked a little guilty. "I admit the excitement has given me unaccustomed energy, but I will retire early too; therefore, we shall not linger over dessert."

The older woman glanced up in dismay, spoon poised over her wine syllabub. When she saw that Katie was quite serious, she ate quickly then rose and followed the two.

"I shall just slip down to the kitchen and make up a posset for you both; nice soothing ones," she called after parting from them in the hall.

Another difference between life in the country and life in town was that the latter moved much more swiftly. Alianora discovered this almost immediately as Katie whisked her from shop to shop to warehouse to bazaar, insisting that she have this or that article to appear well, holding up bolts of cloth—merino, kerseymere, muslin—with colors ranging from white to primrose to pale blue, although Katie ended by rejecting the white. Alianora needed some color to offset her pale skin and hair. That did not apply to the court dress, of course, which must be white. Alianora herself chose some darker colors for pelisses and riding habits: blues, greens, and violets.

It was a windy spring day. The air was so fresh and crisp that between the absence of the soot/garbage odor and Katie's intense enthusiasm, Alianora found herself enjoying the outing immensely. The shops were, admittedly, quite crowded, but the people were friendly. Katie noticed just how friendly her acquaintances were, especially those mothers of hopeful sons when told that Alianora was the daughter of an earl.

"You see," she exclaimed as they walked out to the waiting barouche. "We shall receive many more invitations now that everyone knows we're here. Why, I believe we shall not stay at home one night for the entire time."

This was not terribly appealing to Alianora, but she resigned herself to it, saying instead, "That will not tire you?"

"Oh, my, no. I feel quite well." She laughed and clutched at her bonnet as a gust of wind threatened to remove it.

"Too windy for my taste, lamby," Mrs. Bowman said as a footman helped push her up into the carriage. She sat down with a whumph. "Enough to give a body a violent chill. Is that wrap warm enough?" she asked Katie.

Katie pulled up her Norwich shawl letting the beautiful border spill over her arms. "Yes, it is quite warm enough, although, Alia, you must note that the fashion is to be as delicately clad as possible."

"I have noticed. It seems highly unreasonable to me. Are people in town not as susceptible to ills as those in the country?"

"Why, yes, they are, but to be fashionable is worth the risk."

"By Saint George," Alianora said, using one of her father's expressions and shaking her head in amazement.

They stopped at a milliner's and spent some time choosing bonnets, some with the new materials in mind, some entirely frivolous. Alianora emerged from the shop, struggling to tie the bow of a new poke bonnet when a sharp gust of wind whipped it out of her hands. She watched in dismay as it rolled over the cobbles, bouncing like a child's hoop. A hand touched her arm and she jumped. It was Lord Savernake. He smiled and bowed.

"What an inconvenience this wind is, to be sure. I have sent my tiger after your bonnet." He indicated a small man running and grabbing unsuccessfully at the recalcitrant article. "It would be a shame to ruin one of Madame Fleur's fine creations."

Alianora looked after the tiger completely unaware of how the wind had put a colorful bloom in her pale cheeks, a sparkle in her blue eyes, how the sun turned her hair to spun gold. Lord Savernake did not fail to notice.

"You have been shopping this morning?" he asked politely.

"Yes, an extraordinary task. It would seem that we will keep all shops in business after this morning." She looked back at Madame Fleur's, wondering what might be keeping Katie and Mrs. Bowman.

"I imagine I shall be seeing you at many balls then and insist that you save a dance or two for me —as a friend of your brother." He waited for her assent, his eyes widening with the conversational effort. She seemed unusually inattentive and he began to wonder if perhaps her mind was not all it should be. "May I drive you somewhere?"

"Oh, no. Thank you, my lord. I am with my sister-in-law," she managed to say, indicating the barouche she was about to climb into.

"Ah. I did not imagine you to be alone here. May I have the honor of calling at William's for you? Perhaps we could drive in the park?"

There was no Lord Cerestone to rescue her this time.

She looked up at him. "Yes, perhaps, sometime."

He was quite relieved. What a struggle it had been to bring her to this point! "I shall call for you then."

Fortunately, Katie and Mrs. Bowman emerged, placing bandboxes in the care of the footman. Lord Savernake's tiger ran up with a slightly dirtied and bent bonnet and Alianora thanked him. Katie greeted the earl cordially then pushed Alianora ahead of her into the barouche.

"I suppose he will be haunting our doorstep," Katie sighed as they moved away. "One cannot deny him. He has entrée to the highest circles, but he is quite a—a *rake.*"

"A rake?" Alianora asked, not liking the sound of that.

"A heathen," Mrs. Bowman supplied.

"Yes, he is a devil," Katie said with a slight smile.

And I am bedeviled, Alianora thought with a sigh.

"A heathen," Mrs. Bowman repeated, diving into her favorite subject. "Gambled away a fortune, now he's hunting for another. Mark my words, lamby." She patted Alianora's arm. "He's not to be trusted. 'Tis a shame, though, a terrible shame to waste such fine looks on such a libertine."

"Cousin Sarah!" Katie admonished but could not help agreeing with her.

Sarah Bowman stiffened her lips and nodded emphatically, saying that what she said was what she meant. Alianora told her of Lord Savernake's invitation and Katie looked thoughtful, saying nothing. In fact, she wished William were here to guide her. She could not refuse Lord Savernake her house—should she refuse him Alianora's company? She would write to William immediately.

Their last stop that day was Hatchard's in Piccadilly to acquire the latest in Gothic novels for Katie.

"You must read them too, Alia," Katie told her. "So that you may speak knowledgeably to anyone. That will not brand you as a bluestocking but as someone who is au courant."

"Oh," Alianora said with a serious look that spoke volumes for her true opinion of this fashion.

"Everyone passes through here at one time or another. You go there to be seen that you go there."

"Then, I am to understand, that people do not go there because they find pleasure in reading?" Alianora asked in amazement.

"Oh, no. Few people would pick up a book unless compelled to do so," Katie told her complacently.

Once inside Hatchard's, Alianora was introduced to the owner, John Hatchard, dressed in his usual

severe black frock coat. He expressed sympathy at
Katie's loss but remarked that she was looking well.
She and Alianora then circulated, leaving Mrs.
Bowman to snooze in the barouche. Katie found
many friends to speak to, moving on toward the
reading room where Alianora met Lord Palmerston
and was forced to admire a rare enameled snuffbox
from Brazil, where she met a number of literary fig-
ures who were arguing languidly around a table,
pointing to an article in the *Morning Post.*

"One once could meet Lord Byron here," Katie
sighed. "He was quite often to be seen in the afternoon—before he left for foreign parts."

"Who is Lord Byron?" Alianora asked and a
number of heads turned in her direction.

Katie hurried her away to where they might col-
lect their purchases, saying she would acquaint
Alianora with the details of Lord Byron later and
that she must not again admit that she knew nothing of him. Alianora promised.

They met three of Katie's friends as they were
leaving: Mrs. Rathbone, Miss Totheringham, and
Lady Eliza Ribbesdale who had all come out with
Katie some six years earlier. They chattered in the
entranceway, completely oblivious to the people
struggling to enter or leave the building, making
dates to meet for tea and comparing notes on which
balls to attend.

Alianora looked at each of them, remembering to
smile only when Katie nudged her, thinking that
each looked like a species of exotic bird. One wore a
satin-ruched bonnet with a fruit garden on top; another had long feathers curling up and back like a
crest; the third had cornered the warehouse on lace
with a bonnet rivaling Mrs. Bowman's for constant

movement. It reminded her of how strange and uncomfortable she'd felt while trying on headgear earlier.

It was a game, she told herself. A game with so many rules that it was impossible to know them all. And, breaking even the smallest of rules led to being gossiped about. Gossip was something, Katie had informed her, that one might indulge in, but at all events one must avoid being the subject.

Katie signaled that they were ready to leave and the two of them walked out, driving off just as two young men paused outside the bookseller's.

"Double it, my dear boy," said the first. He looked after the barouche, lifting a Malacca cane in the head of which was embedded a quizzing glass.

"I say, isn't that—? By Jove, it could be," he said. "But with my less than perfect vision, perhaps not. Hal, that barouche that just departed the shop, was that not the Wynyate gal inside?"

The other young man swung around and stared. "Familiar, yes," he agreed. "Yes, believe so."

"Ah, then. Shall we wager on the outcome when she meets friend Cerestone?" the other offered.

Henry held out his hand. "A side bet. Cerestone will be first to be legshackled."

Alianora met with the dancing instructor later that afternoon. The furniture of the small drawing room had been pushed to the walls and Katie had recruited the butler to play the pianoforte. Dancing was something Alianora truly enjoyed. The medieval dances—admittedly more Tudor than medieval —were no less complicated so she learned the new steps rather quickly: the various sets, the movements in the columns, the swift step called the "lovers' knot," the fifth variation in the quadrille called the "flirtation," which involved a continuous exchanging of partners.

The dancing master was a tall, lanky Frenchman who spoke little and criticized, in the main, with the movements of his thick eyebrows. Alianora learned that "up" meant she had executed a step he had never encountered before; "down" meant she had done something completely wrong; "sideways" meant that perhaps she would do. After a succession of "sideways," she began to feel quite comfortable, even with the waltz, which was, in her experience, a little too intimate. She did enjoy the dizzy, flying sensation it created as they twirled about the room.

Before an early supper, she spent the evening in the garden, listening to the birds and watching the sunset, letting her mind roam to the easy solitude and magical atmosphere of Grassmere. After supper, she joined Katie for her first lesson in whist and penny loo.

A cool, sunny morning found Alianora dressed in an amethyst velvet surcoat, split up the sides with a long train for riding. Underneath she wore a rose linen gown and snug top boots designed by her father. None of her new riding habits had arrived as yet. She had thrown open a window and a fresh breeze gently lifted the gingham curtains and ruffled the blue and white toile bedclothes.

Sitting before a dressing table, she frowned at her reflection. She had never paid much attention to her appearance before—being far more concerned with comfort because at Grassmere she spent a great deal of time outdoors. Being so closely confined with

Katie, who thought appearance a vital concern, one could not help but become conscious of it.

She slowly brushed her hair, pulling it over her shoulder so that she might plait it. In truth, she had no idea of the standards of beauty. Her father had always said she was pretty enough without adding folderols. Her mother, who everyone declared to be beautiful, had told her she was lovely.

She peered into the mirror, suddenly deciding to braid in a green satin ribbon. Could she also be beautiful, even though she was completely unlike her mother? Or was she, in truth, quite plain? She had such deep blue eyes, such pale hair. Was that good or bad? She had never wondered about it before. Nor did it truly matter, she decided, not when she could go riding in the park and enjoy the spring day.

Finishing the braid that hung down to her waist, she stood up, pulled on her gloves, and left.

With an undergroom trailing her, Alianora rode down the street, adjusting her knees to the unfamiliar sidesaddle. She sang a little, nodded at an herb seller, a baker pushing his cart of wares, a girl with new strawberries to sell. All the merchants turned to stare at the exotic sight that rode past them, then with a comment on the odd tastes of the aristocrats, they returned to their labors.

What a pleasure it was to gallop this frisky mare across the dewy spring grass! The cool wind whistled past her ears, polished her cheeks. Few people were abroad so she rode easily anywhere she wished, half the time allowing Hypatia her head. When Hypatia tired, Alianora set her to walking, moving in among elms to the banks of the Serpentine. She dismounted and led the mare along behind her, finally handing the reins over to the under-groom.

Before her, on the lake, a black swan and her cyg-net swam gracefully toward Alianora, with open bills as if expecting to be fed.

To Alianora's left, a little up the bank in the shadow of the trees, a small girl in a Bath chair tossed out chunks of bread to the swans. The girl looked up when Alianora walked toward her.

"These are my friends, Lady Black and her baby, Miss Sygnette," she said and giggled.

Alianora nodded, sitting on a stone bench nearby. She had never had trouble speaking with children. "They are both quite beautiful."

"Yes. And these are my friends, Lady Jane and Princess Alianora." She presented two dolls from among the colorful myriad of shawls that covered her. Lady Jane had dark curls and Princess Alianora had long blond hair decorated with scarlet ribbons.

Alianora looked at the dolls then at the little girl in surprise.

"Alianora," she echoed.

"Oh yes. My brother told me Alianora was a mid-evil princess who lived in a castle on an island. He said he saw her on his way to London but that is hard to believe, is it not?"

"Yes, I think so," she said with a smile to herself.

"Oh, I didn't mean to be rude. I am Fanny. My brother is a viscount, Lord Cerestone." She spoke most proudly.

"Lord Cerestone," Alianora repeated.

"But you have not told me your name," Fanny pressed.

"No, I haven't and that is quite rude of me. I

wonder if you would believe me?" She laughed. "I met your brother last week. He is quite handsome."

"Yes, he is."

"We were celebrating Saint George's Day when his coach broke down. He stopped to visit with us. Do you know who Saint George was?"

"Oh yes. Peter tells me lots of stories, especially when I am sick. I was sick this past Christmas and Mama says I am not recovering as I should."

"I am sorry to hear that. Perhaps all this sunshine will make you feel better. I often have the headache myself, especially when I must be among a great crowd of people. My mama sometimes makes up a special tisane." She looked around, frowning a little. "Are you alone here?"

"Oh, no. Tavvy, that is, Miss Tavisser, my governess, has run off looking for Bobbin." She wrinkled her nose. "My little brother."

"I have a little brother, although he is quite grown now. He was very mischievous too." She retrieved one of the shawls that slipped off Fanny's lap. How lonely this little girl seemed, bright and personable, and yet only swans and dolls for friends. She was unusually serious for her age, which Alianora guessed to be ten or eleven.

"I have not yet told you my name," she said and smiled. "It is Alianora."

A snort came from the shawls. "Nooo. That is a faradiddle."

"A faradiddle?" Alianora questioned but thought she understood. "No, it is quite true, I assure you. My name is Alianora and I do indeed live by the river, although our castle is now, unfortunately, in ruins."

"You can't be Alianora. She isn't real."

"Oh, I am quite real. Here, take my hand, touch my sleeve." The small hand that reached for hers was quite fragile and cold.

"But that doesn't mean you *are*," Fanny objected with the merest hint of doubt in her voice. "I don't mean to be rude."

"No, you aren't. It is difficult to believe, I think. Do I match your brother's description?" she asked with a laugh, pulling her long braid over her shoulder.

Fanny stared at her. "A little, perhaps," she allowed. "But my Alianora is a princess."

"Ah, there you have me. I am only the daughter of an earl."

"My Alianora plays a harp."

"She does? Now, that is a true coincidence. I play an instrument called a psaltery, which is not unlike a harp."

"But you don't have it with you."

"No, the days of strolling troubadours are past, I'm afraid. Aside from that," she added, glancing back at her mare, "I don't believe Hypatia would care for such strange noises coming from her back."

Fanny giggled. She cradled her yellow-haired doll and said to herself, as if quoting someone else, "Alianora has gossamer gold hair as if the pale dawn light came to rest on her head."

"What a beautiful thought," Alianora said in amazement and considered the source: Lord Cerestone. The thought warmed her and a part of her suddenly wanted very badly to be the Alianora so described. She picked up her braid. "Perhaps it would appear to be more 'gossamer' if I unplaited it."

This appealed very much to Fanny who nodded

vigorously. She watched as the loosened hair spilled in waves over Alianora's lap and onto the bench. Alianora shook her head and smiled at Fanny, awaiting her judgment.

"It *is* gossamer!" Fanny cried. "Oh, may I comb it, please?"

"Do you have a comb?"

"Oh yes. My Alianora always needs to have her hair combed."

Alianora obligingly presented her back, pushing all her hair back over her shoulder. She was prepared to endure the jerking and pulling of inexperienced hands, but Fanny's touch was surprisingly smooth and light. It was so relaxing that she could easily have fallen asleep had the bench not been so hard or cold even though it was in the sun. After a while, Fanny announced that she was finished and Alianora complimented her on her skill. She then re-plaited it.

"Do you come here each morning?" she asked as she worked.

Fanny nodded. "Miss Tavisser likes to let Bobbin run about because he is so very lively."

"Would you like for me to come by again to see you?"

"Oh yes! That would be beyond anything. Could you—could you bring your salt-ary?"

"I could. Perhaps you'd like to learn to play it too?"

Fanny agreed, looking brighter and more enthusiastic than the sad little girl Alianora had first encountered. They were interrupted by the return of Miss Tavisser looking quite bedraggled but triumphant as she dragged a small boy behind her. A large dog, introduced as Hector, immediately investigated Alianora then woofed and wagged his feathered tail, ready to play.

Alianora introduced herself and Miss Tavisser said that she hoped Fanny "had not been too troublesome."

"Not at all. She is a lovely person." Alianora asked if she might visit Fanny again and, Miss Tavisser, after looking down at the small pleading face, agreed.

Alianora smiled at Fanny. "You see, I am also new in town and have few friends."

Miss Tavisser pushed her other charge forward. "This is Master Robert."

Master Robert looked up at his governess and grimaced then stared at Alianora.

"You are dressed funny," he announced.

"Bobbin!" Miss Tavisser said sharply. "Your manners! Please excuse him, my lady, he is particularly full of himself today."

"I have a younger brother too, a little older than Robert, perhaps, but he was once a terror around the manor." She held out her hand. "I am pleased to meet you, Master Robert."

He hesitated, then shook her hand very fast, then ran behind Miss Tavisser, peeking around her skirts. Alianora laughed then signaled her groom to bring the mare to her. She used the bench as a mounting block and, with a wave, rode back through the trees.

"What an odd person she is, to be sure," the governess muttered, thinking she would just check with Lady Cerestone to be certain Lady Alianora was not *too* odd.

Fanny looked after her new friend. "She is *my* Alianora."

Chapter Six

Alianora stared down in horror at the carriageway quite six feet below her as the perch-high phaeton moved smartly along. The vehicle was so high that she had been obliged to climb a ladder to enter it. Lord Savernake was, of course, not about to allow Alianora, or any feminine passenger, to leave the phaeton precipitously. To that end, he let his right arm lay along the folded hood, resting tight against her back, his hand loosely gripping her upper arm. He handled the reins competently, using the whip to advantage when needed, removing his protective arm only for that purpose.

Alianora found the carriage seat too narrow, having moved as far as possible from the earl, and still his thigh pressed rather too insistently against hers. She sat forward a little, stiffening her spine, making an uncomfortable ride even more uncomfortable. She gripped the top of the side panel and braced her feet against the dashboard, remembering as she did so Katie's troubled look and Mrs. Bowman's blunt disapproval of this outing.

"He's not to be trusted, lamby," Mrs. Bowman declared. "Why, you're no more than a babe and he's a worldly heathen."

Katie admitted she could not like the idea of Alianora riding in such a vehicle.

Alianora sighed helplessly. "I should not have accepted his invitation."

"Well, truly, I believe no harm can come of a simple outing in the park. You need only be civil and polite and refuse to go anywhere private with him."

"I wish now that I had not agreed."

Katie smiled a little. "It would be impolite to refuse him now. If you truly do not wish to go in the future, refer him to me." There, that was unequivocal. She would wait to hear from William before saying anything further.

Alianora shook her head. "It is a problem I must face myself, rather like bearding the lion in his den, or pulling a dragon's tail. After all, I must learn to resist the heathens of the world, mustn't I?" They both laughed.

No, Alianora decided as the early afternoon breeze set the plumes on her new bonnet fluttering, sent clouds overhead scudding across the sun. No, she did not care for Lord Savernake's insistent familiarities. Was all his attention leading to a proposal? She hoped not but could not deny the possibility. It was too bad that her father liked him so well for she simply could not tolerate this man. But she could not say so directly—that was not part of the Marriage Mart game. She must do all in her power to discourage him without losing one ounce of civility in the process.

Lord Savernake had been all this time speaking of his vehicle, calling on her to admire the fine japanned body, blue picked out in gold, and the high-stepping matched chestnuts, how responsive they were to his commands, how skillfully he tooled the ribbons—refuting Lord Cerestone's jibes at Grassmere. He spoke of others in the park, how well he knew them, and shared some light gossip. At times he halted by the side of the tanbark to speak to those strolling along or riding by; sometimes he pulled alongside another carriage for a short way. Alianora greeted all his friends and acquaintances, wondering a little at some of the intense stares and the way some seemed to point and put their heads together. Perhaps that was simply the way city people were. She did wonder, in this tall vehicle, what might happen if, in all this stopping and starting and visiting, one team crossed another's path? And what might happen if the huge rear wheels of the phaeton should catch the wheels of another carriage or worse, simply *fall off.* It truly frightened her and she tried not to think of it.

Savernake was comfortable, admiring the color of her eyes when he glanced at her. She seemed a positive dunce in society, but he would require no more of a wife than her fortune. She could remain in the country all her life, leaving him free to pursue his former life-style. Once again, this morning, the nasty advent of bailiffs had awakened him from a restful dream of riches.

"That is quite a pretty rig you're wearing," he commented, knowing that a woman, slow or not, loved flattery. He did wonder briefly if she would even understand what he said, then decided that he was too severe.

"Thank you, my lord," she answered, thinking that she really must do something about his grip on her arm. She kneaded her new reticule. Inside she could feel a neatly folded handkerchief, a vinaigrette box that Katie had insisted she carry, a paper of pins for hasty repairs, a comb, and a steel looking glass. She moved her fingers over and over the items, thinking. She lingered over the pins.

She appreciated his compliment because, in truth, she did like her new carriage dress. It was of an ice blue tricot de Berlin with two flounces resting neatly on the tips of her white kid sandals. She wore a white velvet pelisse painted along the hem and front borders with bouquets of pink, purple, and yellow spring flowers. On her head sat an Angouleme bonnet with a blue satin ribbon tied in a bow beneath her right cheek. Admittedly, her new outfit made the clothes she wore at Grassmere seem quite plain. That did not, however, distract her from her consideration of how to stop Lord Savernake from touching her so intimately. She held on to the paper of pins, nodding to herself. One more move on his part and she would stab him. *Direct action.*

Unaware of the violence in his companion's heart, the earl continued musing on his comfortable future. He would, in truth, marry an heiress whose countenance could frighten a mastiff if it meant rescue from the duns. And Lady Alianora, fortunately, was striking in her own way. He would leave her in the country while he pursued his own happiness in town. Such a lovely thought. He glanced at her pale face and smiled, dark eyes glittering.

At that moment Lord Cerestone tooled his curricle into Hyde Park for Cressida's third driving-lesson. He was not happy. Either his cousin was naturally obtuse or deliberately so as she had hardly, as yet, even learned to hold the reins properly.

Of course, she was being deliberately obtuse. Cressida smiled at her cleverness. How else did one catch a man but by proving how helpless one was, thereby evoking his manly instincts? She peeped up at her cousin from under the brim of her conversation bonnet admiring his manly form. She took every opportunity to press closer, every jounce, every pit into which the wheels dipped found her clutching his arm for support, letting her reticule dance over his buckskin-clad thigh.

After stopping and speaking to a number of acquaintances who were all invited to admire Cressida's new plum silk habit, the viscount found a stretch of Rotten Row relatively free of traffic. Once more, with an exasperated patience, he threaded the reins through her fingers.

"I believe I have it now, Peter," she assured him, letting her hand linger within his. Her look was one of innocence.

"Yes, even Georgina could tool the reins after three lessons," he told her with a level glance.

She was immediately all enthusiasm, knowing that she could push him no further. A spark of anger lit her blue eyes quite briefly, but the bonnet hid it.

"Do not," he reminded her, "allow the ribbons to fall. Keep them taut or the horses"—he indicated the dancing grays—"will run away with you."

She nodded seriously, closing her parasol and laying it at her feet. Numerous plum and black plumes tickled the viscount's nose and he struggled not to sneeze. He hardly noticed when Cressida set the grays deftly in motion.

He survived the struggle, puffing at the feathers whenever they struck his face. It pleased him to see that Cressida was trying harder, his goal having succeeded. She even managed to drive and speak at the same time.

"Georgina will be quite amazed," she observed. "I must invite her to go driving quite soon, that is, when she has recovered from her come-out. I am quite looking forward to the ball and have ordered a gown that is *sans pereil*. Why, you shall not know me at all I shall sparkle so! Not, of course, that I wish to put poor Georgy in the shade, but then it will be her ball so I daresay no one will notice me. Oh, there is Mary Brumleigh! Oh, Mary!" she called with a wave, swinging the hand with the ribbons to the right.

The grays objected to this sharp pull, snorted, danced to the side of the carriageway. Pedestrians scattered quickly. Cerestone took her hand, warned her sharply to move her fingers not her whole arm when signaling the horses, and then brought the curricle back into line. Cressida, with ready tears on the tips of her lashes, promised most adamantly that she would do everything the viscount told her. He gave in, consoling himself with the thought that he would only be subject to this trauma a few more times before declaring her "trained" and setting her loose. Naturally, he would not be in the vicinity when she demonstrated her newfound skill to the beau monde.

"How few people there are abroad! I am all impatience to drive at the fashionable hour." She looked up at her cousin, tears forgotten, a coquettish smile on her face. "Peter."

He knew that wheedling tone and glanced at her in a sort of horror.

"You know, Peter, I will be needing a carriage of my own to drive," she told him. "And horses, of course. I should like to cut a dash myself and need someone to help me." When he did not answer, she pouted. "Please, Peter, *please* will you order a phaeton for me? I will tell you what would please me. Peter!" A tiny frown creased her forehead.

Cerestone, however, had spied Lord Savernake's ridiculously high sporting phaeton ahead of them.

The woman beside the earl, her features in profile, he recognized immediately. *Alianora!* He had heard from Fanny that she was here in London but had not encountered her anywhere. One could say he was studiously avoiding her if one were truthful, but one rarely is. He forgot Cressida completely.

But Cressida, intensely sharp and jealous where other women were concerned, was not about to allow his attention to wander. Who was this rival? The viscount had whispered some odd name, but she did not catch it. She spoke to him. He did not respond. Well, she decided she would show him. With a smug smile, she dropped the reins.

The grays, always working right up to their bits, took immediate advantage of this freedom and increased their speed.

Cerestone began to realize that something was amiss when the curricle lurched to one side, narrowly missing a barouche. The dowagers in the barouche screamed in unison and one pounded on one of the grays with her parasol, thus encouraging them into a gallop. Cressida shrieked and clutched at the viscount, her plumes completely obscuring his vision. He tried to put her from him but she clung like a limpet and over the dashboard went the reins, disappearing beneath pounding hooves.

The curricle bounced and jounced and lurched. Someone shouted "Runaway!" and the cry took up all along the circle. A rather rotund major yelled "Tally-ho!" as they passed and spurred his surprised mount into action. Several young bucks thought it quite a lark and joined in the chase.

Cressida panicked and screamed in Cerestone's ear. He tried desperately to shake her loose so that he might jump onto the off-side horse but she was beyond reason. She had dropped the whip so he had nothing with which to control the cattle. By the time he yanked out the blinding plumes, he saw that it was too late to do anything. The grays had swung left and were heading for Lord Savernake's phaeton. All he could do now was hang on to Cressida and the curricle.

Lord Savernake, still speaking easily to Alianora, glanced at her and just managed to catch a glimpse of the swiftly approaching vehicle. Recognizing danger, he gripped her tightly about the waist and snapped the ribbons. The chestnuts responded by galloping.

Assuming the earl was becoming amorous, Alianora put her plan into action. She pulled out a pin and stabbed his thigh.

The earl released her with a howl. It was then that the curricle hit.

Fortunately, the grays had swerved so that only the wheels were entangled. But the force was such that Alianora lost her grip on the panel and tumbled out and down into the curricle, landing rather nicely in the viscount's lap. The advent of Alianora into the curricle tipped it alarmingly, however, and pitched Cressida out into the dirt where she landed on her derriere. Unhurt, she immediately stood and shrieked at her cousin, conveniently forgetting that it was she who was at fault.

Lord Cerestone looked at Alianora, his eyes full of concern. "Are you all right, my lady?"

She looked at him and smiled. "A little bruised, perhaps," she said. "It was quite a surprise."

"I had hoped to meet again but not so—precipitously."

"Do you drive this badly?" she asked, beginning

to think about exactly where she was and becoming a little uncomfortable.

He laughed, a short bark of ironic laughter. "I was, unfortunately, teaching my cousin Miss Finsbury the fine art of tooling the ribbons. In the end, it is my fault."

"Cerestone!" It was the earl. He stood by the curricle. "You are not fit to drive a dog cart!"

Cerestone gently moved Alianora to the seat beside him. "Oh, certainly, my lord. I can drive a dog cart."

"You have damaged the axle and upset my chestnuts. I demand compensation."

The viscount's eyes flashed but he was all compliance, nodding as one of the bucks who had followed handed him the ribbons. "Send the repair bills to my man."

Savernake was a little taken aback but, upon looking around at the crowd gathered, he decided to be gracious. Realizing now why the earl had grabbed her, Alianora regretted her action.

"I am sorry, my lord," she said softly. "I—I didn't understand."

He could not afford to be too incensed so Lord Savernake accepted her apology, although at the moment his leg smarted more than his pride .

"I shall arrange for you to be taken home," he told her.

"Never mind, Savernake, I'll take care of Lady Alianora," Cerestone told him, earning a glare.

"Peter!" Cressida shrieked. "You cannot leave me here! I'm hurt! I'm in pain!"

The viscount sighed inwardly. "Come into the curricle and I'll see you both home."

"There is not room," Cressida objected. "You are so cruel. I hate you!"

"Come with us, dear," called one of the dowagers in the barouche. They were finding this more exciting than a Gothic novel. Savernake escorted her to them and they made much of her, which mollified her to some extent.

Lord Cerestone backed the grays up and with the help of the major and some others managed to disentangle all wheels. The curricle was, fortunately, only scraped and some repainting would hide the damage. The viscount signaled the grays with his recovered whip and deftly caught the thong. He looked at Alianora.

"You are not afraid to ride with me?" he asked, a mischievous twinkle in his eyes.

"Well, mayhap, if you promise that we will meet no one else *accidentally.*"

"Trust me." He raised his eyebrows and she laughed, forgetting that she had just been in a carriage accident.

Katie expressed alarm and Mrs. Bowman declared that "it didn't surprise her one bit" when told of the accident. Alianora assured them she was unhurt, with only a minor tear in a flounce. The older woman, nevertheless, insisted that she go right upstairs and rest after a nice hot bath. Katie turned to look out the saloon window after the two left and said softly to herself, "So, Viscount Cerestone."

That night Alianora was able to attend the opening of Almack's. Countess Lieven granted her permission to waltz, bringing a red-haired young man to her. Katie also danced, her brown eyes sparkling.

As uncomfortable as she was with her less than graceful partner, Alianora felt the trip to London had been worth it to see Katie in good spirits once more.

But as she sipped the orange-flavored orgeat and nibbled the small tea cakes, she felt strangely let down.

It surprised her to discover that she looked everywhere for the man with the teasing green eyes—at Almack's, on Bond Street while shopping, in the park, at the booksellers, even when she was presented to the queen.

She'd felt lonely and frightened in the Drawing Room, and realized that her mind fixed on the one person in London who made her feel safe, comfortable. She thought of Lord Cerestone even as the Prince Regent lingered over her hand, remarking on her porcelain complexion, pronouncing her to be the reincarnation of the fair maid of Kent, that worthy Joan, wife of Edward, the Black Prince, who had been considered fair in her youth. Those courtiers who stood nearby repeated the epithet to others until the entire room seemed to be hissing. Alianora rose from her curtsy and then stood, eyes downcast in an agony of embarrassment, her hands clenched together. She yearned for Grassmere.

It was a relief to return to Katie's, but there she found her brother Percy anxiously awaiting her. He had obviously been pacing the drawing room, running fingers through his fine blond hair. His blue jacket was a little wrinkled and his cravat unevenly tied. He grasped Alianora's hands as she entered, taking a moment to admire her Drawing Room costume of large hoops and feathers.

"Lord, Allie, is that the rig you must wear to make your curtsy?"

She smiled although her head was now throbbing beneath piled, powdered hair. "It is as uncomfortable as it looks."

He let go her hands and tried to appear hearty, but his eyes gave him away. "Must have cost a pretty pound."

"Three hundred pretty pounds," she told him.

He looked at her, turned away, then swung back as if he could not make up his mind. "Allie, I must speak to you," he said finally in a voice that was a little hoarse.

"Well, yes. Could it wait until I have changed?" she pleaded, having more than an idea what he had come about. She would go to her room and count out what pin money she had. No matter what his weaknesses, he was still her brother.

And he was almost pathetically grateful when she laid a reticule full of guineas into his hands.

"You know?" he asked, horrified that she could guess why he was here without him telling her.

She nodded. "I have heard you and William arguing."

He flung himself on a sofa, closing his eyes in pain. "I don't know what to do anymore. This is far from all I need, but where to go? William refuses to help. Father gave me some, but I told him it was for a pair of sweet-goers."

"Oh, Percy," Alianora sighed.

"I know. I know. I hate it myself, but my case is desperate. I may need to visit a cents-per-cents in order to honor my debts." He had to explain the slang to her and she was horrified.

"I could ask for more allowance," she offered.

Percy groaned. "I have already imposed enough on you. I must find my own way out of this. Somehow."

"Perhaps I could sell—"

"No! No!" he said, jumping to his feet. He shook the reticule. "This is enough. After all," he added ruefully, "you should enjoy your stay in town."

"I'd much rather be at Grassmere."

"No doubt," he agreed. He walked to her and took her hand. "Thank you, Allie. You've saved me. I'd best go now." He hesitated, a great war going on behind his eyes. "Allie, I must ask one more favor."

"Of course," she said readily and he flinched.

"Please, be obliging to Lord Savernake." He quickly kissed her cheek and left, to avoid seeing her reaction.

She looked after him with a worried frown.

Within the hour she received a visit from Savernake himself, who came to see how well she had survived the accident. He bowed over her hand, looking natty in pale canary pantaloons and blue jacket.

She took back her hand. "I have had no ill effects," she assured him. "Shall you wish refreshment, my lord?" She would be obliging, as Percy had requested. But she would never marry Lord Savernake.

"No, I shall not stay long."

She nodded, remembering Katie's admonition that she must never receive men alone, but she believed this was a special case. She owed him a sincere apology for stabbing him with the pin. With a sigh she sat down, disposing the lavender jacquard muslin about her to discourage wrinkles—another one of the many, many pieces of advice Katie had given her.

Lord Savernake watched her, sitting at ease on a striped confidante, admiring her striking looks and the graceful way she handled herself. More and more he liked the idea of marrying her and with her brother, Percy, now desperately in his debt, he just might succeed with this chit.

"And—and you, my lord, have you recovered?" she asked, meaning more than the accident, of course.

"I have some pain, but not unbearable, I think."

"Oh." She laced her fingers together as if the act would impart strength. "I truly apologize," she said quickly.

Savernake waved a hand, knowing just how much to milk another's guilt and when to finish it off.

"If you are truly sorry, perhaps you'll accept another invitation to go driving with me. This time"— he smiled pleasantly—"we might see some of the sights of London. The menagerie at Exeter Exchange perhaps." The idea sent him into a paroxysm of boredom. He went on to enumerate the delights there, something to entice the slower mind. "There are monkeys, lions, and tigers, and even a hippopotamus." His voice faded a little as he saw her looking at him in her steady, unnerving way once again.

Despite the earl's opinion, Alianora was not slow. She was beginning to understand a little of what was going forward here. Combining what Katie had told her of the earl and what Percy had just asked of her—"please, be obliging"—she suspected that Savernake was the one leading her brother into gambling. But her love was not blind; she knew Percy went along willingly. Then again, he was not happy about it. She remembered the pain in his eyes. Perhaps she could plead with the earl to leave him alone. They could not continue to speak here, however, so she agreed to go with him the following Monday and rose, signaling that the visit was at an end.

All thoughts of Lord Savernake and Percy fled when she discovered her small friend, Fanny Everhurst, was ill. Alianora had missed her in the park for the past several days and had wondered how she was. Lord Cerestone's note that morning told her all she needed to know—that Fanny wished to see her.

Katie could not like the idea of Alianora visiting Lord Cerestone's home, but because it was young Miss Everhurst who had actually requested the visit, and if Alianora took a maid with her . . . And, remembering William's desire that she look about for a husband for Alianora, Katie thought this friendship with Lord Cerestone's sister might lead Alianora to like the brother.

Alianora took little time to dress, waving the maid away, simply pulling on a light sprigged muslin and topping it with a nile green spencer. The thought of seeing Lord Cerestone once again caused her a little difficulty in breathing and, perhaps, she spent a little extra time carefully tucking in loose strands that had escaped from her crown of pale gold braids, but then she turned to what she needed to take with her.

Under her bed lay a chest filled with bagged spices and herbs. She dragged it out and lifted the decorated lid and was immediately surrounded by sweet fragrance. Taking a small pillowcase, she emptied into it pouches of sweet woodruff, rosemary leaves, and lemon verbena, something to help induce restful nights. She picked up her psaltery, knowing that Fanny would ask for it. She left in the barouche, stopping the coachman briefly so that she might buy some daisies from a flower girl, then continuing on.

There was no sign of Lord Cerestone at Hurst House and Alianora felt a small pang of disappointment. She smiled, however, as she entered Fanny's chamber. Everywhere there were daisies, on the bed hangings, the coverlet, the crewel-embroidered chair by the window, the drapes. Fanny had said once that she loved daisies more than any flower. On a side table sat a blue vase filled with purple and pink windflowers. Sunlight fell across a bright gold carpet, picking out the tiny green and blue designs, and lit up the Bath chair sitting in a corner.

"Alianora!" Fanny greeted, propped up on pillows, wispy chestnut curls framing a thin face.

After greeting Miss Tavisser, who said she would leave the two alone for a short while, Alianora kissed Fanny's cheek then sat on the bed.

"Daisies for you," Alianora told her. "Shall I put them in the vase over here?"

Fanny nodded, thanking her most properly. Alianora finished arranging the flowers and then brought out the scented pillow. Taking it with both hands, Fanny held it to her nose and breathed deeply, her bright eyes looking over the edge of the linen.

"This," Alianora told her, "you must place under

your big pillow and you'll have very pleasant dreams." She sat on the bed again. "I have missed you in the park. Lady Black sends her love."

"I've been sick again," Fanny said, with a touch of self-disgust, as if she were at fault.

"Sometimes it is difficult to recover," Alianora told her.

Fanny's eyes strayed to the door as she lowered the pillow. "Peter comes and stays with me so it is truly not so bad. You have your psaltery?" she asked eagerly.

"Why, I believe I did bring it with me," Alianora said in surprise. She picked up the instrument, laid it across her knees, and unwrapped the purple velvet cocoon. She brushed her fingers across the strings.

Fanny's eyes were wide. She reached for it then pulled back her hands with a sheepish look.

"Do you remember the way to pluck the strings?" Alianora asked, referring to the times they had worked with the instrument in the park.

Fanny nodded vigorously and she was able to pluck out an entire song before her fingers began to stumble and she yawned.

Alianora smiled sympathetically. "I should be leaving, my sweet *burde,* so you may rest."

"No, please, not yet," Fanny begged. "Sing for me."

"Well," Alianora hesitated, glancing toward the door. Miss Tavisser had not returned. "If you promise to close your eyes."

Fanny agreed, pulling her dolls to her chest and hugging them. She closed her eyes obediently.

Alianora looked at the thin, waiflike face and felt

she could almost cry. It didn't surprise her that Lord Cerestone would forgo all entertainments in order to stay with his sister. She only wished she could do more. Plucking a few introductory chords, she began to sing a ballad about three ravens.

Chapter Seven

Lord Cerestone yawned over his *Morning Post* in the library. When Alianora began to sing, he looked up then leaned back and closed his eyes, letting the strain of the past few days recede a little as he listened. He couldn't hear the words of the ballad, but that clear, soft voice soothed him.

His mind roamed freely over the past weeks in town, lamenting the terrible upset to his routine, not that one would find him admitting he was such a creature of habit: the neglected books, neglected manuscript, the lack of time for contemplation. He cringed at the thought of the interminable evenings spent squiring Georgina and the Finsbury sisters to various balls, breakfasts, to Vauxhall, to the Haymarket; the time spent escorting his stepmama on her infrequent outings. And his friends! He'd seen them only occasionally, one crisis after another causing him to send his excuses.

Not that he begrudged the time spent with Fanny or even with Georgina nor did he regret having met Lady Alianora, though it was she who had overset the comfortable tone of his life most of all.

He'd never been given to dreaming, rather his life had been devoted to reason and facts. Now he suddenly found himself reading the same page twenty times while his mind was far away. And of what did he dream? Of a maid with golden hair, laughing in the sunlight as her hawk returned to her hand, singing old ballads in the candlelight, dancing in ancient costume with such grace . . .

"Peter!"

He came awake abruptly. Cressida Finsbury stood before him, her brown ringlets topped by a fetching little feathery bonnet. The blue eyes beneath the brim were annoyed. Beside her stood Georgina dressed in a simple russet walking dress with double frills at her wrists and throat. He had to admit that his sister did have style and seemed positively conservative next to Cressida's flashy volatility. He frowned, presenting a severe expression to the girls, but neither quaked. The viscount looked at Georgina wondering if, perhaps, he'd been a touch unreasonable with her in the past.

"Good morning, Cressida, Georgina," he growled, reluctant to let go his reverie. He noticed that the singing had stopped. Hector, who had been lying at his feet under the table happily accepting bits of muffin, raised his head and woofed once.

Cressida cringed but held her ground. She knew she was in Lord Cerestone's black books, at least ever since her display of temper in the park, which had been ill-thought out but, of course, she allowed, there had been unusual circumstances so she wasn't entirely at fault and he should understand that. And he had been so tied down with the sick Fanny that there'd been no occasion for them to further their relationship. She took that opportunity now—it was knocking—and tried the sympathetic approach.

"Peter," she said with a sad smile. "You do look tired."

"I am."

"I've truly missed our lessons; however, I am happy to wait until Fanny is recovered."

"Generous of you," he observed shortly.

Well, she thought so, especially in light of his rudeness. He was not responding to that particular approach so she switched to arousing his jealousy.

"Lord Savernake, you know, has offered to continue the lessons himself." She watched for his reaction.

He merely cocked a dark eyebrow. "How generous of him."

She pushed it a little further even though Georgina tugged at the sleeve of her pelisse.

"He has been so kind as to say he would help me design a carriage—one to suit my particular coloring."

The viscount looked at her. "Do not place too much value on his attentions. He is well known for his profligacy."

This was more like it! She smiled and the result was bedazzling. Peter, however, would not be dazzled.

"Georgina, do not linger over your shopping. Fanny will need the powders from the apothecary this afternoon."

"I know that, Peter," Georgina told him indignantly. "I have been ministering to Fanny as well as you and entertaining Mama at any time this past week."

He smiled apologetically. "Yes, you have, and I appreciate your help."

She nodded. They were interrupted by Alianora who appeared in the doorway of the library.

"Lord Cerestone," she said with a slight smile. "Miss Tavisser said you wished to see me."

"Yes." He put his paper aside and came to her. He looked at Georgina and Cressida, amazed at how he seemed to forget the world about him when Alianora was near. He at least had the presence of mind to introduce the three of them.

If Cressida had been Hector's counterpart one might have observed the hackles bristling; as it was, she looked Alianora over with a slight lift of her eyebrows. Georgina, sensing her friend's hostility, tempered her own greeting, although she had no reason to dislike Lady Alianora and could only appreciate her help with Fanny. Alianora stared placidly at them all, amused at Cressida Finsbury and struggling, at the same time, to still the rapid beating of her heart in Cerestone's presence.

Moving to the viscount, Cressida threaded her arm through his and looked up at him.

"Peter, I would infinitely prefer you to continue teaching me," she said silkily. "I cannot wait until we may go out together again."

He looked askance at her. "I cannot say when that might be."

"I may wait for you after all, I believe." She glanced at Alianora. The bonnet's brim hid her smug smile from Lord Cerestone.

"You are of age. You are free to do as you wish." He gently but insistently removed her arm from his. "I suggest you leave for Bond Street as the time is fleeting."

Cressida didn't like his dismissal nor did she care for his reference to her age, but even she could see that no more could be accomplished at this time. Again the thrust of the bonnet hid her expression from him. She glared at Alianora as she swept past, leading Georgina from the room, and repeating the sobriquet the Prince Regent had bestowed upon the visitor, "fair maid of Kent," as if it were something to be ashamed of, something to be ridiculed. She then laughed in a way that might have delighted her admirers but seemed merely malicious to Alianora.

Alianora lifted her chin. Miss Cressida Finsbury certainly appeared to harbor an excessive hostility toward her—but she was no threat to Cressida's relationship with Lord Cerestone, or was she?

Alianora still stood near the doorway clutching her purple-wrapped psaltery, afraid to move as she looked into Cerestone's wondrous, kind eyes, afraid to shatter the moment. Again she was alone with a man, but in her life at Grassmere she had never been so followed about by maids, footmen, and grooms so she accepted their absence without a qualm. He was so handsome, the embodiment of a young King Arthur. She remembered dancing with him in the banqueting hall, how quickly he learned the complicated dance despite his denial, how interesting and lively had been their conversation. And, more recently, the accident in the park when she had landed in his lap—how she had been content to remain there even in full view of the public! The thought caused her to blush, which brought Peter to himself at last.

"I am being rude, I fear, my lady. Please, sit so that we may speak," Lord Cerestone said, indicating a comfortable leather chair. He sat opposite her. "I wished to thank you for coming to Fanny. She treasures your friendship."

Alianora smiled, looking down as she smoothed the velvet over the instrument. "She is quite special."

Tired of waiting for the next muffin-fall, Hector stood up and shoved a cold nose under his master's hand. Finding nothing, he left for the nursery where Bobbin might be taking his mid-morning tea.

"I hope you will feel free to come at any time to see her," he said, watching as the tail disappeared out the door. He then looked at Alianora, the crown of golden braids, the graceful tilt of her head, the long, slender fingers.

She raised her eyes and he admired the clear, deep color, the open, honest countenance—her emotions there to be seen and read. She now frowned a little, looking worried.

"Will she be all right? It is nothing—mortal, is it?" she asked.

"The doctor believes she will eventually recover. Quite often delicate children grow into perfectly healthy adults."

"I do hope so. I will do all I can to help her. Would it be permissible to come every day?"

He held his breath. To see her every day, in his own house—he would never accomplish a thing. Perhaps it would be better to remove to his club each day she visited or arrange to be away escorting Georgina or his stepmama somewhere. But how could he allow such an opportunity to escape him— to see her, to listen to her beautiful voice? It was a dilemma—the sort of internal debate he never engaged in. The solution was always one way or another, completely unequivocal. He kicked himself mentally. He would return to his old life, finish the manuscript for his publisher—John Murray had already prodded him this week, reluctantly arranging a new due date. He would leave town in less than two months and settle back into his comfortable life at Woodhurst. That decided, he sat back in his chair.

"Yes, please come as often as you wish," he told her, breathing at last. "However, do not curtail your own activities for Fanny, I beg you. She will understand."

"There is nothing so important that I may not at least see her once a day," she assured him, becoming a little more relaxed.

"I have an invitation for you to Georgina's ball. We're firing her off next Tuesday." He brought it out of his pocket and handed it to her. "For you and your sister-in-law, of course. I hope you will be able to come."

"I shall consult with Katie," Alianora said with a laugh. "We are so busy it has been truly inconceivable to me. I know of no obligation, however."

"I believe the ballroom will be decorated in the manner of a classical circus: swags and swags of greenery, material draped from the ceiling as if we were all under a tent. Georgina and her mother are planning it. I have merely to show up."

"Shall I come as chariot driver or lion tamer?" she teased.

He laughed. "Perhaps Athene to bless the games or Terpsichore to lead the song and dance." He indicated her psaltery.

"Well, I shall be quite demure," she resolved. "After all, it is to celebrate your sister's debut into society."

"She is already quite celebrated. After the ball, our knocker shall never be still, I fear."

"More opportunity for her."

"Too much opportunity may give one a headache."

They were interrupted by Beeley, who carried a tray of refreshments. The viscount apologized for his lack of manners and gave the butler an appreciative nod.

Alianora stood. "Oh, no. I cannot stay. I must send for my maid."

Beeley bowed. "I shall have her attend you immediately, my lady."

She thanked him. "I hope that the ball will not be too much of a trial, my lord."

"Only a tribulation at worst." He had come to his feet as soon as she did and moved closer to her.

Suddenly uncomfortable, Alianora moved away toward two glass-fronted bookcases. They were ceiling high, topped by wooden pediments and owl finials, flanking a large window. She glanced over the titles, noting the preponderance of "Histories of . . ." Nestled in among Moroccan-bound, gilt-lettered books was one whose author was quite familiar. She turned with a questioning look and found Lord Cerestone standing behind her. He smiled.

"Yes, I am afraid I did write that dusty old tome."

"May I?" Alianora asked and he nodded. She set her psaltery aside and carefully pulled out the volume. "Being the history of Tudor household economics and their effect on ensuing history, with special notes on the Clerks of the Green Cloth," she read aloud. "How, uh, interesting."

He chuckled. "It was at the time; however, I

would never wish to sift through the household accounts of anyone again, not even someone as fascinating as Henry VIII."

"Then you truly have spent your life between the pages of a book."

"I stand accused, sentenced, and committed, my lady."

She smiled to herself, that impish, internal smile that positively intrigued him. Shaking her head, she replaced the book, closed the case front. He was disappointed when she did not take his verbal bait then wondered at himself. Why should he assume she would? They had met not above three times and barely knew one another, yet it was so easy to slip into the same camaraderie he shared with Buck and Henry. That was a bad omen.

Her maid came and she left and Cerestone returned to his paper. After some time of reading without comprehension, he laid it aside. It felt as if the sunshine had gone away.

Alianora returned to Katie's, hugging the psaltery to her as she entered the hall. Upstairs it sounded like company in the drawing room so she decided to slip past until she saw Katie lying rather limply on the sofa. Mrs. Bowman and Katie's friend, Lady Ribbesdale, fluttered about her.

"Katie," Alianora said. "Are you all right?"

"Oh, Alianora," Katie said a little faintly, her face pale. "I was a trifle dizzy." She smiled. "Too many late nights I am afraid." Color gradually returned to her cheeks and she sat up. "I feel much better now. And I promise I shall rest this afternoon."

Alianora put the psaltery on a nearby table and

joined Katie on the chaise, taking her cold hands between hers. "Shall I help you to your room?"

"Thank you, but I truly am better." She looked up at her friend. "Thank you, Eliza. I am sorry our tea was cut short."

Eliza, formerly of the fruit-garden bonnet, nodded worriedly. "Then I shall leave you to the care of your family. I'll drop by tomorrow to see how you are getting along."

A footman led her downstairs. Mrs. Bowman poured a cup of tea for Katie.

"Here, lamby, tea will restore you."

Alianora looked at the older woman and asked, "What happened?"

"Just a spell, I'm thinking. Plenty of rest and tea and she'll be right as a rain shower."

"Yes, yes." She sipped from the cup. "Now, tell me, Alia, how is Fanny? When she is better we should have her to visit."

"Lord Cerestone assures me she will recover." Just speaking his name made her feel warm inside and, thus distracted, she missed the significant looks that passed between the two matrons.

"Yes," repeated Katie. "I should like to meet her."

Alianora smiled. "She is so intelligent and sweet. I hope that I may see her walk while we are here."

"I wish that too. And, now," she said, putting down her cup and saucer, "I believe I shall retire. No, no, Alia, stay, please, and receive any visitors. Cousin Sarah will see that I am tucked in."

"Of course, lamby. Let's go." Mrs. Bowman placed a large, soft arm about Katie's waist and off they went.

Alianora sat for some time thinking how the wonderful city life and city air seemed decidedly unhealthy for some people. They should all return to Grassmere where the wind brought clean, crisp scents from the land and river.

The next day Alianora remained at home to take care of her sister-in-law, singing to her and reading a truly awful Gothic novel that Katie seemed to revel in. Katie approved their attendance at Georgina Everhurst's ball and insisted that Alianora have a special gown made, something in a blue to match her eyes. She would give her a delicate sapphire necklace to wear with it. Never mind the pearls that society dictated for young girls. Pearls disappeared against Alianora's fine skin—sapphires would do very well! She insisted that Alianora keep the necklace.

Her mother wrote that all was well. The earl had wandered away only once thus far and was discovered on the road to London, declaring that he had "thought to visit his daughter at court." Alianora smiled a little mistily. Belisande was in full molt, according to Stephen, so he concentrated now on training several of the other hawks. Spring was in full bloom at Grassmere, the days were warm and fragrant, and everyone missed her, missed her singing about the place. She sighed, longing to be home.

Alianora found an hour to visit Fanny, who was sitting up in bed and, happily, seemed to be gaining strength. Lord Cerestone was absent from the house the entire time and Alianora left feeling quite disappointed. But then, she would certainly see him Tuesday next at his sister's ball.

Later that day she received a disturbing note from Percy, saying that he would be gone from town for a few days and she was not to worry. Not to worry!

When she knew he owed some vast amount of money! The last sentence left her in an even worse state. *Lord Savernake will speak to you of it when next he takes you driving.*

That would be tomorrow. Yes, she would speak with Lord Savernake about Percy. It was too bad to take such advantage of another's weakness!

Monday Katie was quite her cheerful self once more and insisted on shopping with Alianora for the Everhurst ball. They discovered a marvelous shade of gentian blue crepe for her gown and decided upon white velvet ribbons with silver spangles for the high waist and small sleeves. Katie insisted that if she would not consent to having her hair shorn she should at least style it a little differently. They consulted with a coiffeur, who waxed enthusiastic over such beautiful hair and said he knew precisely what to do. Why, she would inspire others to adopt a longer style!

They returned in time for a small nuncheon. Katie said that she felt sleepy and would take a nap. No, no, there was nothing wrong.

Alianora went upstairs to change for her ride with Lord Savernake, allowing the maid to dress her in a primrose carriage dress with matching spencer trimmed with bright green frogs and braiding down the sleeves. When the maid left, she stood for a long time looking down into the garden, noting how the sunlight glistened on the new leaves of the plane trees, set the patches of daffodils aglow, sparkled on the small lily pond. She would rather be there, sitting on the stone bench listening to the thrushes and robins than driving out with someone she loathed.

Lord Cerestone. She let the name linger in her mind as she contemplated the oasis of nature. The thought of him surrounded her like a warm hug; his smile and twinkling eyes left her a little weak in the knees as she pictured him. If only she were to drive out with him! He made her feel comfortable, and safe, and imposed neither his will nor his presence upon her. She thought of the ball and smiled thinking that they would, perhaps, have a chance to dance together again. And after the ball—? The thought suddenly chilled her. Would she see him again? Surely, if she continued to see Fanny he would be at the house once in a while. The next thought horrified her: Could she return to Grassmere knowing she would never see him again?

The maid entered and announced that Lord Savernake awaited her below. It took Alianora a moment to clear her head and return to the present. Yes. Percy. Time to slay Percy's dragon.

Lord Savernake rose when she entered the drawing room, immediately complimenting her upon her appearance. With Lord Cerestone she might have riposted with a phrase such as "did he mean her looks or the fact that she had arrived at all?" It would not do for Lord Savernake.

He was handsome in his own way, his costume flawlessly pressed. Katie had told her of town beaus who required two men to help them into their coats. Alianora thought that quite impractical. Could one ride comfortably, sit comfortably, reach out to catch a hawk?

He bowed and led her outside where she saw, to her relief, a curricle rather than the phaeton awaiting them.

"I thought we might take a turn about the park

and then a brief ride in the country, stopping, of course, at an inn for refreshment. Would that please you, my lady?" he asked, settling beside her and signaling the footman to let loose the horses' heads.

"That will do, my lord," she said, her voice cool.

He turned to look at her, not certain how to interpret her words, then decided she simply meant she agreed.

Unfortunately, Alianora had no chance to mention her brother as they stopped and chatted with a number of people out enjoying the afternoon in the park. Perhaps she would have an opportunity at the inn where it would be quieter and she could face him. She would then tell him she was not interested in seeing him again and that he must leave Percy alone or she would report all to William. It gave her a pang to think that she might be betraying Percy, but he truly needed help to disentangle himself from this well-dressed octopus.

After two passes through the park, Lord Savernake turned the curricle toward the Stanhope Gate and they were soon on their way out of the city, neither having noticed the raised quizzing glass—zebrawood finishing in a gold ball—taking note of their departure, nor having overheard the worried words addressed to a rather stocky horseman in natty brown nankeen. The two men hurried away to Grosvenor Square.

Alianora herself felt quite uneasy as they left the crowds behind. Lord Savernake occasionally passed a farm wagon or slow coach, driving along at such a spanking pace that she feared for her new bonnet. She tightened the bow along her cheek then gripped her reticule. She still had a paper of pins.

They at last pulled into the yard of a small tavern

shaded by tall chestnuts still dropping blossoms. An ostler appeared to take the horses and Lord Savernake helped her alight, letting his hands linger on her waist as he did so. With an insistent wiggle she freed herself, declaring that she was positively parched and nothing less than a pint of ale would quench her thirst. This served to raise Lord Savernake's eyebrows and tickle him into a disgust, as she had intended. But he shrugged it off, believing that a little ale might make her more amenable to his proposal—not precisely her intention.

Savernake joined her just inside and led her to a private parlor such as it was in such a little place. There was a table bare of cloth, several rickety chairs, a bench with dusty cover beneath the one small window. It smelled musty and damp despite the dry, windy day. A boy in a dirty apron appeared in the doorway and Savernake ordered ale for her and brandy for himself.

"Not the best in accommodations, perhaps, but the spirits are adequate," he said, inviting her to sit. She did so very gingerly.

"Lord Savernake," she began, but was interrupted when the boy returned, setting down the mug of ale so roughly it slopped over. She picked up the mug, let it drip a moment then sipped from it. Dutch courage, she knew. The ale was strong and bitter but then she was accustomed to the mead her father brewed.

"Lady Alianora," Lord Savernake said after finishing his brandy. He sat opposite her at the table, twirling the glass between his fingers. "I have brought you here for a reason."

"Yes, my brother, I believe," she told him. "Percy

sent me quite an odd note saying that you would explain his predicament to me."

"I am afraid I must tell you he is quite deeply in debt; in fact, he has repaired to the countryside to escape the duns. Should they catch him he'll be thrown into Newgate."

Alianora gripped the handle of the mug very tightly. "You have led him to this, have you not, my lord?"

His dark eyes widened at this soft attack. "Not entirely," he admitted. "Your brother asked to be led."

"I know that he has the gambling fever. But he is young and merely lacks proper guidance."

"You are fortunate that I am his primary creditor for I have a solution that will satisfy everyone, I believe."

She waited, trying to still the fluttering in her stomach. He smiled at her, but the friendliness failed to light his eyes.

"I am prepared to forgive all his debts to me and arrange to cancel the others if you will consent to be my wife, else," he sighed, "Percy must spend quite some time in debtor's prison."

"How much does my brother owe?" she asked after a moment.

"You could not begin to pay, my lady."

"Perhaps not, but together with my elder brother, William, we might reach some arrangement."

"Percy would not accept help from William," Savernake told her simply.

"You are right," she agreed. "Let us then be reasonable."

He smiled. "Reasonable. Certainly. Simply give me your assent and all shall be taken care of. You hesitate." He rose from his chair, tall and lean, and walked to the window. "I shall then list the advantages of marrying me. You may have observed my sense of style, my skill in conversation. I am not unhandsome and retain some popularity among the highest circles. You would be free to remain in the country while I visited the city at various times of the year." He tilted his head, smiled. "There. You see, I am quite reasonable. I might also add that I do know precisely how to bring a woman to ecstasy with my touch."

Alianora watched him in fascination during this self-congratulatory recital.

"Still, she hesitates," he sighed, as if a woman should swoon at his words.

"You possess a remarkable opinion of yourself, my lord," she said in amazement. The thought of Lord Cerestone ever saying such a thing almost brought her to laughter, but she schooled her face to a cool expression. "But I can—"

"Perhaps," he interrupted, "this will convince you at last." He was not pleased with her hesitation. He had never had trouble convincing heiresses to accept him; it was the avenging mamas, or brothers, he added, who ruined his plans in the past. This was the first time he had an heiress in his hands who had no protector. At this moment he could even kidnap her if he chose, but that was a last resort. From his coat pocket he pulled a letter sealed with red wax.

"From your brother," he told her.

She took the missive and broke the seal. Inside, in rather shaky copperplate, Percy apologized for his weakness, stated his great fear of going to prison, begged her not to report his problems to William for she "knew how William could rail at one," and pleaded with her to fall in with Lord Savernake's plans for the earl had agreed she might remain at Grassmere while married to him. Her life would not change substantially in any way and Lord Savernake was not such a bad fellow, was he?

For a time she held the letter, unseeing, then laid it down on the table not noticing how it soaked up the spilled ale. Did she have a choice? Oh, Percy! How could he ask such a thing?

Taking advantage of her confusion, Lord Savernake thought it time to show her a little of the delights in store for her. She would certainly not refuse him then. He helped her stand, removed her bonnet, deftly pulled out the pins that held her braids in their coronet. When he began to loosen the plaits, letting his hands brush over her face and neck, she came to herself.

"My lord, no! You may not do this," she said angrily. "Even were we to marry I would not allow this—this intimacy."

"Surely, you would not see this as a marriage of convenience?" he told her in a rather silky voice. "You have had no experience in physical pleasures between a man and a woman. Let me introduce you."

She had no experience in refusing men's advances —there had never been the slightest need at Grassmere. Every man there had known her from childhood and respected her as the daughter of her father. Even the visiting knights, with the singular exception of Lord Savernake, treated her with the greatest chivalry. Chivalry was what she was accustomed to, a respect for her person and her desires.

She had tried to be polite and indirect as Katie suggested, but it had not succeeded.

She pulled away, glaring at him. He was surprised at the desire she sparked in him, rather magnificent in her anger, blue eyes flashing, the braids, partially undone, sending forth rippling waves of gilt over her shoulders. It would please him tremendously to take her above right now, anticipating the wedding. Her stance told him it would be quite a battle, however, and he liked his women rather more willing.

"I shall not require an answer now," he offered generously. "Tomorrow will do, at Georgina Everhurst's ball. Yes, that would be rather ironic."

"That is—this is so little time," she said a little breathlessly. Could she put him off until she discovered another way out of this dilemma? Refusing outright would endanger Percy and her protective instincts came into play. She would try and save him another way, sacrifice her portion. If she remained at Grassmere, she would never need it anyway.

"Perhaps it is very little, but remember," he said with eyes narrowed, "your brother has very little time. I should be forced to reveal his whereabouts to the creditors." And it would soon be time to move again, he thought in frustration, although being seen about town with an heiress had quieted his own creditors for the nonce. "And one cannot predict the dire effect the scandal would have on your father. Only think! There would be no more tournaments. No one would wish to be associated with such scandal for fear of being tainted."

That left her cold. She must protect Percy. She most certainly must shield her father.

"For all this hard work," Savernake continued, "I believe I deserve something. A kiss."

Seeing his intention, Alianora backed toward the door. Where she would go once out of the room she knew not. Perhaps the landlord would lend her a mount. Lord Savernake caught her as she struggled with the door.

"Come," he whispered. "Let us sample a little of wedded pleasures, my love," he ended with no trace of love in his voice, his eyes, or his manner. He pulled back a moment. "You have no pins by you?"

"Pins! Yes!" She grabbed for her reticule.

But her captor was faster. He pushed her against the door and smothered her with his lips.

She felt disgust, felt the rough boards pricking her back, felt his hands as they took great liberties. With an unfeminine growl, she shoved him from her, pulled the door open, and ran.

And crashed into a broad chest. Protective arms immediately surrounded her.

"Oh!" she said with a sigh.

Chapter Eight

"Cerestone, how unfortunate," greeted Lord Savernake, brushing dirt from his coat sleeves and straightening his cravat.

"Heiress hunting again?" said the viscount over the top of Alianora's head. He turned to her, putting his hands on either side of her face. "Has he harmed you, my lady?"

She shook her head. "No, we had merely stopped for refreshment."

"He did not force himself on you?" Lord Cerestone asked, looking again at Savernake.

"N-no. I was frightened by a—by a mouse," she ended lamely, embarrassed at her foolishness in coming here alone in the first place and not wishing to mention anything of her brother.

"You see, Cerestone. A harmless outing. We were having quite a pleasant interlude until you arrived."

The viscount pressed his lips together, eyes as cold and hard as emeralds. He looked from one to the other wondering what to believe—Lady Alianora's fright seemed to come from more than a mouse. He had seen her feed one to her hawk without flinching. He suspected that Savernake had become too friendly but could do nothing if Alianora denied it. And if it had happened, why *would* she deny it? He continued to frown fiercely, although when he looked down at her flushed face his expression changed to puzzlement.

She looked away from him, hating to lie.

"I do say," called a voice from the taproom. "Shall we be going, Cerestone?"

Savernake sneered. "Brought your odd fish friends with you, I see." But even he recoiled before the viscount's flare of anger.

"You should take more care in your words, Savernake," he said softly. "One might take offense. One might then retaliate."

"One could take offense at threats, but one is not fearful today. Lady Alianora," Savernake said, taking up one of her hands. Cerestone could not help noting how she leaned away from him but left her hand in his. "Shall we return to town? I believe our afternoon has been sufficiently ruined."

"Oh, Savernake, did I not tell you? How careless," the viscount said, blinking slowly. "Someone left the stable door ajar and your team is, by now, halfway to Margate. We shall have to return Lady Alianora to the bosom of her family. Rotten luck. It should take all night to find them."

Savernake's eyes glittered with frustrated anger. "I believe you shall pay one day, Cerestone," he warned. "And it will be my great pleasure to make certain you do."

"As you will," the viscount invited, becoming more cheerful. "And, now, my lady, I see that you are missing your bonnet and reticule. Fetch them and we may leave."

She did as he suggested, responding with a small nod to Savernake's "tomorrow" as she passed him.

Lord Cerestone did not smile as he handed her into the landau. He had to accept her word that nothing had happened, although he would never trust Savernake, not with his sister and not with this lady. Unfortunately, Alianora was not his sister, and he had no right to interfere.

Alianora greeted Buck Rasherly and Henry Parkington, asking how they had been since last they met. They exchanged pleasantries as the carriage rode slowly back to London. The conversation lagged.

"I say, Cerestone," said Buck, looking over the landscape with an oversize quizzing glass set in a chased-silver handle. "Was my interference timely at the inn?"

The viscount smiled, the wind ruffling his dark hair. "Quashed my temper."

Buck nodded in satisfaction. "Wouldn't do to duel if one can help it. Nasty business, possibly fatal."

Alianora's eyes widened. Had it almost come to that? A duel? Surely not! Lord Cerestone was a historian not a duelist. He would be killed! The thought chilled her. She looked at him wishing she might thank him for saving her, but that would be admitting she had needed to be rescued—something she had already denied. Would that he would look her way so that she might smile to show that everything was well, but he seemed to find the hedgerows and meadows of more interest. Had he developed a disgust for her after discovering her alone with Lord Savernake? She found that thought intolerable.

"I am quite looking forward to tomorrow's ball, my lord," she said, trying to break the pensive mood.

"I look forward to the following day," Cerestone answered, "so that my life might return to some semblance of normality."

"Waste of time," Henry declared. "Balls, routs, never had such pain in m'feet."

"That is because you jump and stomp about so in the dance that it is a wonder you still have feet, dear boy. You must slide and glide with a minor hop or two."

Henry snorted. "Sliding and gliding—s'for hogs on ice, not human beings."

"And jumping and stomping are for enraged bulls," Buck drawled, turning stiffly and nodding at his friend. "Or a clodhopper."

"Never hop clods, ride over them," Henry told him.

"I beg you, Lady Alianora, tell Mr. Parkington something of the joys of the dance," Buck said.

"Some might find it difficult to execute the steps," she allowed with a suppressed smile. "But I believe the executioner eventually learns to cut a figure."

Buck lost control for a moment and laughed, delicately. Henry brightened and said, "I say!"

Lord Cerestone turned to look at her. "As long as he does not give the cut direct."

"Or cut to the quick," Buck added.

"A mortal wound," said Henry.

"And all because of a simple dance," Cerestone said, shaking his head. "Indeed, Hal, you'd best stay away from the ballroom."

Alianora laughed and they continued to send sallies back and forth until the landau reached Katie's house. The viscount escorted her to the steps.

"I should beware, my lady," he told her softly, "of bad eggs. They are apt to turn on one."

She laid a hand on his sleeve, saying lightly, "I am not yet in the basket."

He took her hand and raised it to his lips. "Call on me should you find yourself so."

She looked up at him, amazed at how her hand tingled beneath his lips. How differently she felt when Lord Cerestone touched her.

"A friend may help a friend, may he not?" he added, his countenance serious, his eyes slightly worried.

She nodded.

"But friends might not always be about when

needed." That was the best he could do without interfering any further.

Gently extricating her hand, she thanked him for seeing her home. He nodded and left as the butler opened the door.

She did not sleep well that night, wishing profoundly that she might speak to Percy before making a decision about Lord Savernake. She sat up in the bed. Perhaps she could find him—no. She lay back down. How would she do so? Only Lord Savernake knew Percy's whereabouts and he seemed disinclined to reveal them.

She sat up again. Perhaps she could insist on seeing Percy first, put off answering the proposal until then. But—no. She lay back down. Time was short. By the following day Percy could be in prison.

Sitting up yet again, she put her face in her hands. How had life become so complicated? She reached out a hand in the dark. Oh, how she needed a friend!

Katie fluttered about, quite excited and in high spirits as they prepared for the Everhurst ball. Her sherry brown eyes sparkled and her dark ringlets shone about her face. She stood just behind Alianora who was seated before her dressing table mirror.

"There! Did I not tell you? How lovely you look! I vow, no man shall be able to resist you tonight."

That was not a cheery thought for Alianora. She wished at least one man might find her resistable.

Katie put her hands on Alianora's shoulders. "Why so sad, dear sister? You shall be seeing Lord Cerestone tonight," she added enticingly.

That brought a smile from Alianora.

"There, so much better. Now, tell me what you think."

Alianora looked in the mirror. Katie had persuaded her to allow her to cut the hair around her forehead and cheekbones and a new fringe of soft curls framed her face. The rest of her hair had been gathered in a knot at her crown with long curls dangling down her back. A silver filigree bandeau sat on her head like a crescent moon.

"It is so different. I think I like it."

"Of course you do! You shall be all the rage. Now, the gown."

She and the maid helped Alianora dress, carefully working to avoid ruining the elaborate coiffure. The gown had arrived only an hour ago—someone had also been awake all night!—and, fortunately, fit perfectly. It was a tunic dress—with an underfrock of white crepe and the tunic of gentian blue moiré, draped and caught at the shoulders and waist with silver-spangled ribbons. On her feet she wore white velvet slippers. Sapphires Katie had given her were set in a silver parure around her neck.

"Gloves and shawls and then we must be leaving," Katie said, stopping before the mirror to puff out the sleeves of her plum silk gown, pressing flat the gold braid on the square neckline. "You are the living image of a Greek goddess, I vow!" she said as they descended.

Sarah popped out of the dining room to admire her lambs, causing Alianora further embarrassment. Alianora had already attended several balls—something prior to the Season, Katie had told her—and danced the waltz at Almack's, but this was her first true ball of the Season. She managed, however, to

hide her fears from Katie. After all, would she not
be seeing Lord Cerestone? Could she not enjoy the
ball just a little before she gave Lord Savernake her
answer?

Katie was speaking as they rode to Grosvenor
Square, lighthearted chatter, that she had heard
from William only the day before and that he might
be able to come to town sooner than he had hoped.
The words faded in and out until Katie mentioned
Lord Savernake, saying that William hoped his sister would not see too much of him, that Savernake
was not a desirable companion.

"But do not let it distress you," Katie quickly assured her. "There will be so many men about tonight that you shall not, in all likelihood, even see
him."

Alianora wished only that could be so. The coach
began to stop and move forward, encountering a
good deal of traffic in the square, but it was not long
before they were able to alight. They ascended the
steps to the ballroom and waited with a number of
people to pass through the receiving line. Alianora
met Georgina's mother, Lady Cerestone, and encountered Georgina herself in high good looks,
dressed all in white with primrose ribbons and
pearls. Lord Cerestone stood nearby, dressed in a
dark blue coat of superfine, white dimity waistcoat,
and breeches of drab kerseymere. His cravat was
modestly tied, of a sparkling white lawn in the folds
of which rested a diamond. He took her hand in
greeting.

"Ravishing, my lady," he said softly.

She felt shy all of a sudden. "Thank you, my
lord."

He smiled. "Are you as nervous as I am?" She nodded. "May I claim two dances immediately?"

"A host's prerogative?" she questioned.

"A host's pleasure," he said, signing her card. "I hope you enjoy the ball."

She left to join Katie who was with her friends. They immediately complimented Alianora on her gown and her hair, their friendly words adding to her self-consciousness. She glanced about the ballroom, noting the primrose material draped from the ceiling as if, as Lord Cerestone had suggested, they were indeed inside a huge tent. Pine swags dotted with white roses hung from the musicians' balcony, were wrapped about the freestanding Ionic columns, and framed the doorways. There were masses of potted palms. Mirrors hung high on the walls reflected the candlelight, making the room quite bright. There were so many people! Alianora was amazed. Everyone moved about constantly from group to group, talking, laughing, plumes waving, jewels sparkling, perfumes wafting through the air like invisible ribbons.

She relaxed a little when the one person she so dreaded seeing did not appear to be there. At least not yet. Men began to cluster about her, bringing friends who wished an introduction and a dance. Buck Rasherly signed for a contredanse as did Henry Parkington.

The receiving line dissolved and the musicians began tuning their instruments, finally breaking into a minuet, the favorite opening dance of the Prince Regent. Lord Cerestone led his sister to the floor and they danced alone for a few minutes— Georgina Everhurst's introduction to society. Alianora saw only Cerestone, how he moved with such grace, how proud he was of his sister. Candlelight brought out the gold sheen of his dark hair and highlighted the planes of his face. With his broad shoulders and lean body he seemed more athlete than historian. He handed his sister to another and those engaged to dance moved onto the floor, including Alianora with a Lord Fitch.

She danced each dance, gliding with Buck, hopping with Henry, twirling with others. Katie took part in a few dances then retired to the wall with her friends, Lady Ribbesdale and Miss Totheringham, fanning herself rather vigorously. It was getting warm, Alianora noticed, but she worried about Katie's health. She asked Katie if perhaps they should leave.

"No, no. I am very well, I assure you. I would not miss this ball for the world."

Alianora wondered a little at her insistence on the ball's importance but agreed to remain.

"As long as you are all right, dear sister," she said. "Tell me the moment you wish to leave, please, even if I am on the floor."

Katie waved her fan and smiled brightly as Alianora's next partner arrived.

"My lady," said Lord Cerestone with a bow.

They moved in among the waltzing couples, whirling in a way that made Alianora feel light and breathless.

"Have you lost some of your nervousness, my lady?" he asked, smiling down at her.

"A little, my lord, although I have never enjoyed crowds."

"It is too bad that we will not be ending the evening with a song as you do at Grassmere."

Her eyes grew a little distant. "There is no place for it here."

"I believe you are right. Fanny has missed you."

"How is she? I have not seen her for two days."

"Much improved," he sighed. "She worries greatly about her friends in the park."

"Ah, Lady Black and progeny. Yes, I saw them this morning swimming merrily in the lake. I believe they miss her, too." She looked away toward Katie and saw instead Lord Savernake prowling along the edge of the dance floor. She stiffened involuntarily.

Following her gaze, Lord Cerestone said, "He shall not hurt you as long as I am here." He frowned. "Unfortunately, he has befriended my cousin, Cressida, who insisted he be invited."

She tried to mask her unhappiness, but the evening had suddenly gone flat and sour.

Sensitive to her nuances, Cerestone wished she would confide in him, and asked her what was wrong.

"There is no need to worry, my lord. I am simply concerned for my sister-in-law who has not been particularly well these two weeks."

He took a deep breath and said no more. Alianora knew he did not believe her, but she would not risk her friend in a duel. She had already made up her mind anyway.

The music stopped. As it was the supper dance, the viscount led her into a dining room filled with small tables. Buck and Georgina joined them as did Henry and Lady Morfey, a widow from Ireland who was rather well known for her fine Andalusian horses.

Cerestone introduced her to Cressida's older sis-

ter, Jane Finsbury, and left them together while he
fetched some refreshments for them.

"I have wanted to meet you for some time," Jane
confessed with a shy smile, "although I was not certain who you were. Cousin Peter says you are remarkable. We must speak sometime so that I may
come to know you." She rose. "I must return to my
mother right now for she has another young man to
introduce. She does not know I am already engaged," she whispered, putting a finger to her lips.
She rose after inviting Alianora to call and threaded
her way across the room.

A little amazed, Alianora looked after her. She
sensed that Jane Finsbury would make a good
friend. Miss Finsbury obviously cared for Lord
Cerestone and that immediately put her in Alianora's good books. She listened a moment as Buck
spoke with Georgina, while Georgina gazed up at
The Walking Stick with admiration. Henry spoke to
Lady Morfey with enthusiasm about his estates.
And she listened, nodding, interjecting her own ob-
servations. Alianora sighed, wishing she might simply enjoy the evening, a young girl in her first Season who had only to think of finding a husband—
even that would be preferable to her worries now.

Not far away, to her right, sat Lord Savernake
speaking with Cressida Finsbury, both of them
turning at intervals to stare at her. She felt her head
begin to throb, an ache behind the eyes that only
sleep seemed to cure. Sleep and her mother's tisane.
She thought of Grassmere and she suddenly wanted
to cry, wanted to go home to her father's world, her
willows by the pond, to Belisande and Geoffrey,
away from the crowds and confusion of London.
But it would be cowardly to run away now. She

breathed in deeply, slowly. Life was not fair. One must recognize the fact and make the best of it. By the time Lord Cerestone returned, she was almost herself again.

"A little of everything," he told her, setting the plate before her and sitting down. "I know that young ladies must appear to eat nothing and that is why so many of them faint—gracefully, of course."

"You need not fear for me, my lord. I was raised to eat properly and well." But her actions belied her words, for she merely pushed the food about with her fork. She was thinking of Miss Finsbury's words, that "Cousin Peter says you are remarkable." She knew he cared for her, but did he—? Was he—? She couldn't finish the question, not with Lord Savernake stalking her like a panther. It would take some time alone to sort out her own feelings.

"The smoked salmon is particularly good," Lord Cerestone remarked. "Don't you care for it?"

"Oh yes, I do like salmon, but I fear I have a headache coming on. Quite predictable, unfortunately, whenever I am in a crowd."

"Would fresh air be of any help? We have a fine garden and the moon is out," he offered.

"Sometimes it helps," she admitted.

"Then come." He stood up, and she took his arm. Neither noticed that others observed their departure.

They walked out onto the terrace and Alianora was amazed at how bright the night was, illuminating the statues and shrubbery and the elaborate marble fountain. The flagstones were cool beneath her slippers, the grass soft and damp.

"It is lovely," she sighed. "I imagine Fanny enjoys sitting here."

"Whenever it is sunny," he agreed.

"I smell roses and another flower, hyacinths, I believe," she said.

They interrupted a couple in mid-embrace, who then ran off, laughing, into the dark. The viscount shook his head.

"It *is* spring," he observed. "When the heart is light and ripe for love."

"A target for Eros," she said with a smile.

"And arrows."

"And bows," she said,

"And beaus," he countered.

They continued walking among trimmed shrubbery and beneath several trees. It was not quiet, but the two no longer heard the noise of the crowd or the music. They were wrapped in the moonlight and the spring air. Silence was a comfortable thing between them and it surprised Peter. He led her to a bench and they sat down, watching the fountain.

"I believe my headache is better," Alianora sighed. "Truly, only sleep rids me of it completely."

"Then it will be gone tomorrow," he said pleasantly. "Alianora," he said, then added, "may I call you Alianora?" She assented. He started to say something, hesitated, then went on. "In the world of your father, that re-creation of the age of chivalry, a knight pledges all manner of odd things for the lady of his heart. He might vow never to eat meat or drink mead, might vow to wear a glove forever or speak only in whispers."

"Courtly love." She nodded as the moonlight burnished her hair. She smiled, a little puzzled at his words.

Once having made up his mind, Lord Cerestone

continued, "Courtly love is not possible between those who are wedded."

"By tradition, no, my lord."

"Peter."

"Peter," she said softly.

The words did not come easily to Cerestone. "When I came to town, I came convinced that I would return to Woodhurst unchanged and continue my studies, ad infinitum most probably." He took her hand in his, the smooth, slender musician's fingers cool and relaxed. "But before I even reached the city, I met you—a medieval maiden of grace and beauty with a voice that can charm a hawk.

"I thought that courtly love would be enough," he continued as she sat very still. He looked at the moon then at her. "I thought it would be enough to admire, to treat courteously, even to rescue the fair maiden, but it is not enough. I find I need you as I need to breathe, that I love you far more than my studies or my solitude." He smiled, his hands cold. "This is sudden, I realize, and you see in me a friend, but I wish to be more. Please, Alianora, say that you will marry me."

She closed her eyes as he rubbed his thumb along her cheek, raised her hand to his lips, then turned that hand to kiss the palm.

"An eloquent silence," he said lightly.

She was stunned, realizing that this was precisely what she wanted, precisely the way she wished to spend the rest of her life—beside the viscount as his wife. She did not need time to think through her confusion. She knew. She loved him, needed him as she needed to breathe. And yet, she must refuse. How could she look into that beloved face that looked on her with such vulnerability and tell him she could not be that life's breath for him?

"It is too sudden," he said sympathetically and she nodded, taking the coward's way out. "Then I shall wait—" They were interrupted.

"Peter," called Cressida Finsbury, and when she came upon them she had a nasty glare for Alianora and a pretty smile for her cousin. "Aunt Susan has suddenly become indisposed. We need you desperately."

The viscount sighed, a sigh from the heart. Too much sherry again. He turned to Alianora. "Shall we go inside?"

She shook her head. "I need a few moments alone."

He nodded, glancing around, as if to slay every dragon of darkness before leaving her. He saw nothing.

"I shall look for you when I am finished," he said, kissing her hand once more. She refused to meet his eyes.

Then she was alone, wrapped in the moonlight, but it was no longer peaceful. It was frightening. Without Lord Cerestone beside her every shadow took on a nightmarish aspect. She could never have imagined this horrible end to her Season—turning away the man she loved, accepting a man she loathed. But she was strong; Percy was weak. Had she been raised differently, sent away to school, isolated from her parents, had they not been so loving, she might have found it simple to turn away from her brother.

She thought of Percy as a child: how he had bravely entered the river and saved her from drowning, she having foolishly entered an old, leaky boat intending to sail about Old Grassmere. He had not even known how to swim! Their rides together on Geoffrey, bareback, barefoot, kicking in the careless way of children to urge the old plowhorse to a faster pace—she remembered them well. The fishing expeditions, the summer days of playing knights and ladies at the castle ruins—what had happened to him? Was it the city? Katie seemed unwell here, Percy had succumbed to terrible temptation, and she was miserable.

"I see that you await me," said a silky voice.

She slowly raised her eyes. Yes, it was he, the nightmarish vision come to life. "Lord Savernake," she said coldly.

He sat down beside her. "You should call me Richard, after all. I assume you have decided on the sensible course."

Was this a proposal of marriage? It was disgusting, especially after the viscount's eloquent and loving words.

"You will marry me," he said. It was not even a question.

"Yes," she answered through clenched teeth.

"Well, then, that is done at last."

"With one condition," she added. "That I may see Percy."

Savernake laughed shortly. "That is impossible at the moment. He would be arrested on sight. Perhaps I might arrange for him to come in disguise. It will take some time to settle his debts, you realize, my love."

She winced at the endearment. "I will not stand before the altar until I have seen him."

He sighed. "Yes, certainly, something may be arranged. Now, I believe we might seal our engagement with a kiss."

What could she do but submit? She had already given him permission by agreeing to their engagement. He was not rough but greedy, smothering her with his lips, letting his hands roam. Finally, she could stand it no longer and began to fight him. And then, suddenly, he was gone.

"I will kill you for that, Savernake." It was Lord Cerestone!

Savernake, on the grass, stroked his jaw. He got to his feet, face twisted in anger, then, slowly, he managed to smile.

"I think not, Cerestone." He looked at Alianora. "After all, I have the right."

The viscount looked at Alianora. "What is he saying?"

"I am saying that she has consented to be my wife."

"No!" cried Cerestone hoarsely.

"Tell him, my love," Savernake ordered.

"Is it true? It cannot be."

"It is true," she said in a dead voice, unable to meet his eyes.

"Then he has forced you. Tell me what he has done and I will help you. Please, Alianora."

She couldn't bear his pain. She couldn't bear her own. To cut swiftly and cleanly was the only way.

"He has not forced me. I have chosen of my own free will," she told him.

"There you see, Cerestone," said Savernake, triumph in his voice. "Why, I do believe I have had my revenge on you! Imagine, so simple, and only a bruised jaw to show for it."

"Yes, you have your revenge," Cerestone said, his

eyes turning from bleak to cold. "I cannot believe I could be so mistaken. You must think me a fool, my lady. I wish you joy of each other." He turned and walked swifly back into the ballroom.

"No!" Alianora cried softly and stood up. "Peter!"

Savernake was immediately beside her, his arm about her waist. "Remember your brother, my dear," he whispered.

"I hate you." The words were wrenched from her.

He looked surprised. "My, this is going to be an interesting relationship, isn't it?"

She pushed him away, and left him laughing in the garden.

Chapter Nine

When Alianora entered the ballroom, Miss Totheringham greeted her with the news that Katie had fainted, although she was now awake and able to return home. Alianora was happy to leave immediately. Of Lord Cerestone she saw nothing.

The next few days she stayed close to her sister-in-law. The doctor came and went, pronounced her well except for simple exhaustion. Katie seemed to improve after the doctor's visit, indeed, appeared to bloom. That at least eased one of Alianora's worries. She had heard nothing from Lord Savernake and worried every day that she would hear of Percy in jail despite her agreement.

More time passed and she began to lose weight,

finding herself unable to sleep. A note arrived the next week from Fanny Everhurst, written in a tiny, childish hand, requesting the honor of her presence at the Serpentine the following morning. Sitting by a sunny window in the drawing room, she reread the note, wondering if she should go. Would Lord Cerestone object? The thought of him sent such spasms of pain through her that she considered declining the invitation. She sighed. That would not be fair to Fanny, however. Her psaltery had lain idle all this time; perhaps it would improve her spirits to continue teaching Lord Cerestone's little sister. She wrote a note of acceptance to send later.

"Here, lamby," said Mrs. Bowman, setting down a butler's table laden with biscuits, cakes, and pastries. Placing several on a dish, she offered them to Alianora. "This will perk up your spirits. And a nice dish of tea."

Alianora smiled briefly. "Thank you, Mrs. Bowman, but I—"

"Now, now, don't refuse! You've become far too thin as it is. Why, one great gust of wind and off you'd go!"

"Perhaps a macaroon or two," Alianora allowed with a little laugh.

"Indeed, Alia, you seem greatly troubled," Katie observed from a comfortable armchair. A tambour frame lay in her lap. "I know you are not happy in London."

"No," Alianora admitted. "But I know I shall be returning to Grassmere in less than a month's time."

"We may leave sooner, if you wish, of course," Katie offered. "William will be here in a fortnight."

A fortnight! How swiftly time moved when one

wished it to stand still. She had no desire to face her elder brother.

"And you have not seen Lord Cerestone since the ball," Katie mused. "Has that anything to do with your sad mood?"

It had far too much to do with her mood, but she was beyond tears now. There was only a numb ache.

A footman appeared in the doorway and announced Lord Savernake below. "Requesting Lady Alianora," he told them.

"Heathen," muttered Mrs. Bowman around her biscuit.

"No, Freddy, have Shoop send him away. The nerve, really," said Katie.

Alianora stood. "No, Freddy. I will come below."

Mrs. Bowman and Katie stared at her, then at each other.

"But you will be disobeying William's express wishes," Katie objected.

"William is neither my father nor my guardian," Alianora told her as she followed the footman downstairs, leaving an astonished Katie behind her.

Lord Savernake was in the Blue Saloon, standing at the window. He was dressed in a fine blue coat with large silver buttons and yellow pantaloons, carrying an elegant walking stick. Women appeared to find him handsome, but she could not.

"You have some news, my lord," she greeted.

He smiled, coming toward her. "I thought we had agreed on Christian names, my lady."

"As you will, Richard."

He took her hand, turning it over to place a kiss on the wrist then the palm. "Yes, your brother is well and sends his love and gratitude. There is,

however, the small matter of money. A nasty subject to approach so early in the afternoon. I have
spoken with those holding his vowels. Many are
quite anxious to be paid."

"I have no money at hand," she told him. "Will
my jewels be sufficient? You are free to ask what
you wish for them. Or use them as payment."

"It will be a beginning."

She left him and walked up to her room, taking
her pearl necklace, a gold filigree necklace with diamond chips, matching earrings, and several other
pieces from her jewelry chest, including the sapphires. She gave them all to him.

"As I said, merely a beginning. There is now the
small matter of our wedding. I wish it to be as soon
as possible. I will take it upon myself to send a notice to the *Gazette.*"

She sucked in her breath. That made it seem more
horrifyingly real—the thought that others would
now know. She had not had the heart or nerve to
tell Katie and she quailed at the thought of what
William would do. Surely he would allow her to
return to Grassmere—? And Lord Cerestone. She
had hurt him so badly that he would never forgive
her.

"When may I see my brother?" she asked, her
face impassive.

"When the bailiffs are no longer interested in
him, of course. There is a masked ball Thursday
next, given by Mrs. Blackworth, a particular friend
of mine. If you choose to attend you may see your
beloved brother there in disguise. I should be happy
to escort you, of course."

"Yes, if that is what I must do."

"I shall then procure a special license for the following day."

So soon! She could be married before William arrived! That could not be.

"Since this will be my only wedding, I wish for some family by me," she told him. "And it is so little time to prepare a trousseau."

"You need bring only your portion with you," he said with a little sigh of frustration, taking his curly brimmed beaver from a table and placing it on his head. "And your lovely self, naturally."

"And you agree that I may remain at Grassmere."

"Certainly. And I shall be here. A perfect arrangement. Of course"—he flicked her chin with a gloved finger—"I shall expect to visit my fair maiden from time to time, to remind her that she is married."

"I shall never forget that," she said bitterly.

He laughed. "Ah, life. I believe I feel like singing. Yes, and we must make another appearance together in the park, quite soon. Perhaps attend a ball or two. Good day."

For a long moment she stood without moving then slowly collapsed into a chair. She seemed to have a continuous headache these days.

Alianora apologized to Katie, who said she would accept it only if Alianora agreed to attend the Shelbys' musical soirée with her that evening.

Katie smiled. "I cannot tell you how many have asked about you. You see, some word of your talent has preceded you. Come, Alia. I know you always feel better after you sing."

Alianora could not deny it.

"And perhaps Lord Cerestone will attend. I truly believe he is quite smitten with you."

Again Alianora remained silent. She sighed, acceding to Katie's wishes, recognizing that Katie was determined to steer her from Lord Savernake.

Dressed in an apricot crepe gown, its square neck edged with a ruffle of gold lace, Alianora entered the Shelbys' large drawing room behind Katie. She was introduced to the hostess, who was happy to welcome another performer. Already a number of guests were standing about, talking; some turned to stare openly at Alianora. In response, she slipped behind a potted palm and closed her eyes, clutching the velvet-covered psaltery to her chest. A footman passed by and offered to relieve her of the instrument, but she refused emphatically. From her hiding place she could see a dais on which were placed a pianoforte and a harp. She closed her eyes again, wishing it would all be gone when she opened them.

"Come, Alia," Katie said, startling her. "Take my arm and you'll feel more comfortable."

Alianora opened her eyes. It was all still there. *Coward,* she thought. This behavior is unworthy of the earl's daughter. You must face your dragons, even if they are only social ones. *Selfish,* she scolded herself, looking at her sister-in-law. Katie asked such a little thing to make her happy.

"Do not worry, my dear," her sister-in-law said as she led Alianora toward the rows of seats, "you will not be the first on the dais. I believe there are several harpists, and several singers, including one who is said to be second only to the great Catalani."

They were stopped by a number of Katie's

friends, who all expressed a desire to hear Lady Alianora sing, looking pointedly at her purple burden. As the friends spoke, Alianora absently scanned the crowd, relaxing only when she caught no sight of Lord Cerestone. He would be more interested in lectures than music.

The hostess rapped for attention and all guests began taking their seats.

"Alia," Katie whispered as they sat down, "you have no jewelry on. I only just noticed. Your black pearls would have done nicely with that gown."

Alianora froze. Her pearls were most likely in the hands of a pawnbroker by now. She finally said in a small voice that she had forgotten to put them on.

Katie took the blame. "It is my fault. I should have seen it earlier." Her words fed Alianora's guilt. "Never mind. It will be overlooked when they have heard you sing."

Mrs. Shelby introduced the special guest, Mrs. Lamentini, a robust woman draped in blue spangled cloth. She began to sing. Alianora found herself fascinated by the performance of her headdress—the numerous feathers danced, fluttered, and took flight with the force of her singing. Everyone applauded politely when she finished.

There followed one nervous young performer after another. The harp was stiffly plucked, the pianoforte rigidly played, popular tunes sung in tight voices. Alianora hoped that her hostess had forgotten her, but it was not to be. Mrs. Shelby called her to the dais, introducing her as an unusual performer.

A sort of sighing sound followed her and she realized that there were a hundred mouths whispering "Fair maid."

Her hands shook as she unwrapped the psaltery. Katie smiled from amidst the faces, giving her courage to continue. She sat down and listened to the strings, which were ever in need of tuning, aware that the room had grown silent. One song, she told herself, and she would escape to Katie's side. She closed her eyes, played the introductory chords, and began to sing, imagining herself alone beneath her willows at Grassmere.

For a moment, when she had finished, no one clapped. Then someone in the back began and the applause rippled forward. Alianora looked up to see Lord Cerestone standing in the far doorway, and she could not move. Mrs. Shelby appeared and announced refreshments in the library. Everyone was happy to move and stretch. Several people praised her performance but then turned away, saying that it was the oddest song, as if Alianora were suddenly deaf.

Quickly wrapping her instrument, she left the dais and looked about for Katie. But her sister-in-law seemed to have disappeared in the crush. She took refuge behind another screen of palms. Several women strolled by, one commenting, "Lovely voice. Why does she not learn to play the harp?" Another added, "It is the least one might expect from such an eccentric sire," while a third said, "How she expects to find a husband—" There was a ladylike snort. "—no one could find such an antidote attractive."

The voices faded, leaving Alianora quivering with anger. She fought back tears, a resolve that lasted until a gentle hand touched her shoulder. When she looked up into Lord Cerestone's concerned face, a tear escaped. She brushed it away.

"Jealous tabbies," he observed. "All with voices that might appeal to the tom of their species."

Alianora smiled at that.

"Better." He nodded. "Now it remains only for you to face them."

The smile vanished. She looked toward the doorway. "I really do not belong here." By *here* she meant London and the modern world.

"Perhaps not," he agreed. "But not because you are unworthy—more because variety is not the spice of life among the ton."

She moved. "I must find Katie."

"Alianora." His voice held her back, caressing her with her own name.

"No," she said, shaking her head. She would not let him speak of his sister's ball. "No!" she repeated, and he stepped back, frowning.

Slipping past him, she hurried to the library, where she found Katie. She remained by her the entire evening, and away from the viscount.

Alianora wore a riding habit of Prussian blue, a small shako with a black feather, and York tan gloves as she set out for the park, the undergroom following behind with her psaltery. Her hair was braided and caught in a golden coil at the nape of her neck. The fringe of curls about her face blew softly, tickling her cheeks. From a distance Alianora looked fresh and lovely, but a closer examination would reveal the hollows in her cheeks and the slight smudges beneath deep blue eyes.

She entered the park, let Hypatia dance a little and trot for some time before turning to the path that would lead to the Serpentine. The sun shone and the air smelled of flowers and damp grass.

Other riders passed her, several bowing in greeting, which she returned with a nod. She signaled the groom that she wished to dismount and was soon walking her horse to the water.

Fanny sat in her wheelchair near the water's edge, lecturing the birds gathered before her as she tossed pieces of bread. Alianora recognized Lady Black with Miss Sygnette. There were two trumpeter swans and a flock of ducks competing for the bounty.

Handing Hypatia to the groom, Alianora took her psaltery and joined Fanny.

"Good morrow," she greeted with a smile.

"Alianora!" Fanny cried, face alight.

"I was so pleased to hear from you. How nice that you are well enough to visit your friends again. I must say they missed you."

"I wish I might take them with me," Fanny said mournfully. "But Peter says we have enough fowl at Woodhurst and that the queen would not take kindly to losing her birds."

"I would not worry too much, Fanny. Swans are remarkably clever. They know just what to eat and where to find it." Still, his name had the power to cause pain. She pushed it deeper inside. "I have brought my psaltery. Would you like to learn another song?"

"Oh yes. That would be wonderful." She rearranged the shawls about her so that her arms might be free, arms that were still painfully thin.

Alianora laid the instrument in her lap and pushed the chair to a stone bench in the sun. Fanny ran her small fingers over the wood, touching the inlay of mother-of-pearl.

"Is it very old?" she asked.

Alianora smiled as she sat down. "Yes, centuries. It belonged to the great-grandmother of my mother's grandfather." Fanny wrinkled her nose in confusion. "That would be a great-great-great-great-grandmother. She lived in the middle of the sixteenth century. Lady Edith Fancher. I am the first to play it since her time."

"No one else was interested?" Fanny asked as if that were unimaginable.

"Uninterested or lacking in talent such as you possess."

Fanny reverently touched the strings. "I love it."

Alianora frowned a little and looked about. "Is Miss Tavisser after Bobbin once again?"

"Oh, no. Tavvy is at home sick. I'm afraid she caught my cold. Peter is with me today. See? He is just over there throwing a stick for Hector."

She saw him. Her stomach tightened and she felt a little faint for a moment. No! She could not react this way every time she met him. What might have been would now never be and she must accept that. She busied herself showing Fanny a new set of chords to pluck and the rhythm that accompanied the song.

She therefore did not notice when Hector came to visit until that hero was licking her face, his fore-paws on the bench, tail wagging furiously.

"Down, Hector!" ordered Lord Cerestone. When the dog acted as if he were deaf, the viscount grasped the collar and pulled him away. "My apologies, my lady. He is as unmannerly as this brat here." His eyes were distant, as if he spoke to a relative stranger.

"I am not a brat," Bobbin objected, marching up to Alianora. He bowed gracefully for a six-year-old and smiled. "I am a knight and I am curtyus to ladies and quite fearless."

"I can see that," she told him.

"We have been learning to be knights and ladies," Fanny told her. "Peter helped us."

"I should like to joust," Bobbin announced. "Or cut off a dragon's head." He fit actions to words.

"Dragons are rather hard to find these days," Alianora said.

"I shall find one and chop it up and feed it to Hector." He looked quite fierce. At the mention of his name, the dog cocked his head. Alianora looked at him doubtfully.

"Hector may not care for dragon. Do they not eat brimstone and breathe fire? I believe their insides must be quite charred and tasteless."

Bobbin had not thought of this. Fanny giggled. Even Lord Cerestone smiled, warmth briefly lighting his green eyes.

She looked up at him, admiring his severe face, the way the hair curled from under his hat, the graceful way he moved. She wanted to say something, say how sorry she was at the way things had come about, say how much she loved him. But she knew, instinctively, that he would no longer believe her. She was honor bound, honor tied, honor gagged.

"Thank you, my lord, for allowing me to see Fanny," was what she did say.

"I can deny Fanny nothing," he said. His eyes warmed again as he ruffled the brown hair. Fanny straightened it primly. "And she knows it well."

"I have been learning a new song," Fanny told him. "Shall I play it for you?"

"Yes, please do."

Fanny did remarkably well for her first time through. The viscount turned to look out over the water. Alianora could not keep her eyes from him. This might be the last time they spoke, shared something together. Her memories would be like one brightly burning candle in an otherwise bleak existence. She would always remember him thus, handsome and kind, filled with love and humor. Fanny's fingers stumbled and stopped and they both looked at her in concern. She tried desperately to smother a yawn.

"I see it is time to return to the house," her brother told her. He bent and took the psaltery from her and handed it to Alianora. "You have been most patient, my lady."

"Will you come tomorrow, Alianora?" Fanny pleaded.

Alianora looked at Lord Cerestone. He moved to the back of Fanny's chair.

"You may need to rest tomorrow," he said.

"On, no, Peter. I promise I shall be very good and rest today and not complain at all. Alianora is my *friend*, Peter."

He looked at Alianora and for a brief moment pain shone in his eyes. He bent over Fanny. "Then if you are very good and the sun is shining you may come. And Lady Alianora may see you."

They said their farewells, as if everything were quite normal and rational. She watched them until the two children, the man, and the gamboling dog were out of sight.

Did he truly believe she would *choose* to hurt him? Perhaps he did, she thought sadly, given what she had done to him.

* * *

An invitation to tea lay on a salver when she returned to Katie's. Jane Finsbury. She sighed. Assaulted by one of Lord Cerestone's relatives after another, all kindly meant, of course, which would make it difficult to refuse.

"Oh, Jane Finsbury," said Katie, looking over Alianora's shoulder. "She is so remarkably different from her sister, Cressida. I quite like her."

"Yes, Miss Finsbury is nice," Alianora agreed. "She has invited me to tea tomorrow."

Katie tilted her head in thought as she sat down. "I shall be with Charlotte tomorrow. Yes, you must go for you have been far too reclusive lately. It would do you good to visit Miss Finsbury. She is so comfortable."

Comfortable for anyone else, perhaps, but decidedly uncomfortable for Alianora. Miss Finsbury would speak delightedly of Lord Cerestone as she had at the ball, cutting Alianora to the quick with every word.

Her mouth twisted wryly. She might make the excuse that she simply must shop for her wedding or for the costume ball she would attend secretly with Lord Savernake. Stupid thoughts, she told herself.

"I shall send her my acceptance," she told Katie with only a hint of resignation in her voice.

Miss Finsbury greeted her with a smile when she arrived and invited her to sit while she rang for the tea tray. Alianora looked about the room. Everywhere it was yellow—furniture upholstered in yellow and black striped satin, the wallpaper flocked with yellow pineapples, the draperies of gold brocade, a rug of ivory, blue, and red.

"Yes." Miss Finsbury laughed. "This is the Yellow Saloon."

"It is quite pretty."

"Overwhelming at first, but one ceases to notice it after a while." The tea tray arrived and Miss Finsbury poured from a silver urn, begging that they might be on a Christian name basis. Alianora agreed.

"I wanted to invite you here directly after the ball but did not wish to be a pest," she told Alianora, smiling kindly. "Or, at worst, be seen as a meddling matchmaker."

Smiling, Alianora braced herself.

"Peter has told me something of his visit to Grassmere. It sounds quite fascinating. A medieval tournament! How interesting it must have been to be raised in such surroundings."

Alianora admitted that she had rather taken it for granted.

"I suppose one would if that is all one knows. I am certain I took our home for granted and all the visits to Woodhurst each summer and Christmas. London must seem more than strange to you. I still find it quite bizarre."

"It would take some time to become accustomed to it," Alianora said quietly.

"How is Mrs. Cheney doing? Has she continued to improve since the ball?"

Alianora nodded. "Yes. The doctor simply ordered her to be less dissipated and rest more often. She tries to lie down each afternoon."

"Then it is nothing serious. Good."

Alianora shook her head.

"And you? How have you been lately? I do not

mean to pry, but I see the same sad look on your face that I have seen on Peter's. I had hoped that I might be calling you cousin-in-law quite soon. There." She nodded. "That is remarkably forward of me, but I truly mean it. Peter's eyes just seemed to shine whenever you were about and when he spoke of you, why, I could only wish my Andrew might say such lovely things of me!"

Alianora looked down at her teacup.

"You did not, of course, know Peter as a child," Jane continued. "He was always ripe for a lark, I admit, but one would discover him more often alone in the library engrossed in a book, jotting down notes. We always teased him about writing a book one day and so he has, several, in fact. I was permitted to follow him about for I was such a quiet child—not that one would recognize the fact now," she added and Alianora smiled a little.

"He changed for the better at school. I believe Buck and Henry helped him in that. The three of them could conjure up the most amazingly wicked pranks. I was quite envious, wishing that I might go to school with them and have such fun too." She sighed. "But after finishing school, he once more buried himself at Woodhurst amidst a great mound of dusty old books. To live and die there in the library, I believe."

Alianora was forced to set her cup and saucer back on the tray; her hands trembled alarmingly.

"Fortunately, Lady Cerestone insisted that he come to London this Season. She was determined that he find a wife and my aunt can be remarkably tenacious." Jane smiled. "Not that Cressida has not tried to attach him, but they would never suit. She would drive him insane inside a week. Although I love her dearly, she has the temper of a viper. And Peter does like his quiet." She sat looking at Alianora who was very still.

"He does love you," she continued and Alianora looked up.

"I know that," she said softly.

"Something has happened between you. I know it is interfering in the worst way, but I cannot bear to see him so unhappy—nor you, for I would count you a friend."

Alianora looked away and did not see Jane glance over her head to the doorway or her frantic looks—which smoothed into a sympathetic smile when Alianora turned back to her.

"I thank you for your concern, Jane," she said. "But there is nothing anyone can do, not even I. Believe me when I tell you that I, too, wish only happiness for Peter." She glanced at the clock on the mantel and rose. "I must be going."

Jane rose also, glancing at the door. "Please, Alianora, stay a moment."

"Let her leave if she so chooses," said a familiar voice.

Alianora turned to see Lord Cerestone. He bowed coldly. Jane looked from one to the other anxiously.

"I thought if you two could meet in a comfortable place and speak, a happy solution might result," she explained.

"If by happy solution you mean marriage then you shall be disappointed, my dear cousin." How stiff and formal he was!

"Surely, you may work out your problems. No one can doubt you love one another."

"One may doubt a great deal," he told her.

"Wh—what do you mean?"

"Why, that the Lady Alianora has already agreed to wed another. Richard Brendall to be precise."

"Oh." Jane looked terribly stricken. "Oh, I am so sorry!" She looked at Alianora. "Please forgive me. I —I—oh!" With tears welling in her eyes, she stumbled from the room.

Alianora went to follow her, but the viscount barred her way.

"I must go," she insisted.

"Wait. Please. Perhaps it is time we spoke sensibly to one another."

Alianora clutched her reticule. "I cannot think what we might say."

"I can think of many things." He stepped closer. "Friends may speak to one another at any time, on any subject. Friends trust one another."

Words failed her. She could not move.

"Alianora." He said her name as if it were music. "I admit my feelings have not changed. I reacted rather badly at Georgina's ball and I wish to apologize. It was difficult to see you in the clutches of that villain. I should have realized that you would never willingly consent to be his wife."

Her eyes flew to his. Had he guessed? Did he know?

"Only give me the right and I shall protect you," he begged.

"I cannot."

He was so close now that she could smell the light scent of his cologne.

"Then tell me that you love him, that you desire his touch above all others, that you would beg him to do this—" He began to kiss her neck, moving gently but relentlessly to her ear, her cheek. "And this," he whispered huskily, moving on to her lips, his arms circling her.

She held back as long as she could, which might have been a full quarter minute at most. Her arms crept up his chest and around his neck, entangling her fingers in his hair. How soft his lips felt, slow and passionate. How different, how very different from Savernake! When Lord Cerestone desired that she open her lips she did so without thinking. She felt dizzy and light-headed, as if her feet no longer touched ground. Overwhelmed by her feelings, she had no idea how many times she sighed his name or that she spoke of love at all. It was therefore a rude awakening when the viscount let her go. He straightened, gently pulling her arms from about his neck. His eyes were like smoldering emeralds.

"Is it like that with Savernake, Alianora? Do you whisper words of love in his ear?" he demanded.

Her cheeks burned. She'd never felt so—so abandoned before. And it had been wonderful! Her pulse raced, her entire body was covered in gooseflesh. What a horrible time to discover that such a feeling could exist!

"I had not thought you so cruel," she said hoarsely.

He bowed. "All's fair."

"I could hate you for that."

"But you love me."

She did remember whispering that as he kissed her. "But I am honor bound," she said, closing her eyes.

He grabbed her arm and turned her to face him.

"Ah, now, we come closer to the truth. Tell me what he has done! Tell me, Alianora!"

She couldn't. He might then challenge Lord Savernake to a duel and be killed. She had rather have him alive.

"It is a family matter," she managed to choke out. "None of your concern. Peter, please."

" 'Peter, please' what?"

"Please let go my arm."

He did so and waited, breathing deeply, more affected than he cared to admit by her touch, by the tears glistening in her blue eyes.

"Why are you so stubborn?" he asked at last. "You will not turn Savernake off?"

"No."

He winced as if she had struck him. "Then it would seem I must return to courtly love. I will admire my lady from afar, make silly vows in her honor, and," he added softly, running his fingers over her hollowed cheek, "watch her die of unhappiness."

She knew that there were others in this world who had made greater sacrifices than she, giving their lives for their nation, their families, their homes. So many had died to see the French emperor ensconced at last on an island in the South Atlantic. What she was about to do in marrying Lord Savernake was little enough in comparison, but oh, how it destroyed her life! She had only the satisfaction that two men she did love would be safe and her father would not suffer a scandal. For, as Katie had already told her, one did not wish to be the object of gossip!

Lord Savernake—she could not think of him as

"Richard"; it was too intimate—had informed her that the announcement of their engagement would appear within a week. She couldn't tell Katie. She couldn't tell William.

Alianora walked in the garden imagining Katie's reaction should she tell her.

"No! You have surely lost your mind!" Katie would cry in horror. "William will not allow it." William was always to be called upon when Alianora showed her stubbornness. "You cannot have agreed to marry such a man. He is a fortune hunter. He will only make you unhappy."

Alianora had no doubt of that.

She would then nod as if there were to be no more discussion. "Wait until William comes. He will straighten things out. Truly, Alia, you have been acting so oddly lately."

And so on, and so forth.

Alianora shook her head. Confiding in Katie would accomplish nothing. Katie would feel worse than she already did and Alianora would feel worse for having overset her. She paced the garden path, her slippered toes digging into the crushed oyster shells, muttering to herself. It would surely cause Katie enough pain when she heard of Alianora's marriage.

"I have given my word," she told the clump of jonquils. "I *must* marry him."

To that Katie would answer, "Words and promises mean nothing to a scoundrel like Savernake. You must simply tell him you will not marry him."

"Unless he proves he is dishonorable, I must keep my word."

Here Katie would frown a little, her voice full of

concern. "I had rather thought you favored Lord Cerestone."

"I do," Alianora whispered to the yew hedge as she trailed her fingers over the clipped edge. That did not, however, mean she was free to ignore honor, her given word. One might even say it came down to a choice between Percy, her brother, and Peter . . .

It grew chilly as the sun slipped behind the houses leaving a red glow behind. She rubbed her arms, staring at the sky, thinking of all the sunsets she'd watched at Grassmere. There the sky was broad, all its day and evening colors reflected in the river. There it was so quiet, only bird calls and frogs broke the silence. Here there was noise all the time, making it difficult to think, to make decisions. Nevertheless, she walked back to the house, at last, unhappily certain that she had made the right choice.

Chapter Ten

Mr. George Raggett, sharp-eyed proprietor of White's, looked over the trio of gentlemen just settling into the reading room. He had made much of his fortune by personally sweeping the floors each night discovering not a few forgotten counters. The trio were good ton, and certainly enhanced the establishment, but they were such poor players. One might starve awaiting their move to the card room. He greeted them, signaled a footman to them, knowing their propensity for claret, then passed on, nodding to those seated about the room. He brightened at the advent of a true gambler just now handing his gloves and hat to another footman. One could not mistake the fine head of dark hair, the glittering eyes of the hunter. He smiled and greeted Lord Savernake.

Lord Cerestone, meanwhile, stared at the wineglass on the dark mahogany table beside him as Buck went over and over, blow for blow, their morning practice at Gentleman Jackson's saloon.

"My dear Parkington, you could not credit how skillful a blow our friend Cerestone can still land."

" 'Course I could," said that worthy, rubbing his jaw. "Was there. Was *my* jaw."

"Of course you were there, but you are not the most observant creature," Buck observed, finishing his first bottle. He nodded as a footman offered to bring another.

Henry thought this totally inane and merely snorted in response.

"Cerestone might be too much among the pages of history, but he is amazingly capable of milling down anyone he chooses, I believe." Buck looked at the viscount who seemed lost in thought and lifted his quizzing glass, a marvelous piece of work of hornbeam carved into a descending spiral with another glass at the end, a reversible glass or spectacles if one's eyes were quite widely set apart. "I say, Cerestone, your left boot has managed to catch fire."

Cerestone looked up. "What? Oh, sorry, gathering wool, I suppose."

"You might have supplied an entire manufactory by now and here I was touting you to the skies."

The viscount smiled. "A tragedy to miss one of your touts, Buck."

"Being a dead bore," Henry said.

"Better than a live one." Buck leveled his glass at his friend. He moved it back to Cerestone. "I wish I might also wish you happy, dear fellow."

"I *am* happy that you and my sister have hit it off so well."

Buck permitted himself to smile, his gray eyes growing less vague. "Who'd have thought it? Georgy has grown into the most remarkable girl."

Henry roused himself with a rumble. "Might as well announce—plan to pick up the handkerchief m'self."

Cerestone and Buck stared at him, then the viscount said, "Lady Morfey." Henry nodded. "Must be a love match."

"A love of horses match, I believe," Buck countered.

"Well, who'd have thought *that?*" Cerestone shook his head.

"Indeed, dear boy, we came along to protect you from just such a circumstance and here are two of us to be wed. We really must see to you."

Henry agreed, joining Buck with a second bottle of his own.

Lord Cerestone laughed a little. "How ironic."

"Kidnap," suggested Henry.

"Too barbaric, dear boy. We are not Vandals."

The viscount sighed. "Kidnapping is not the answer. The lady has given her word and will stand by it no matter the consequences. What I need do is discover what brought her to that point."

"Too fine a lady to agree out of hand," Buck observed.

"Exactly." Lord Cerestone frowned as he noticed Lord Savernake entering. "Here is my Nemesis now."

"Cerestone," greeted Savernake with the barest of superior nods.

Cerestone looked him over, noting the sparkling diamond pin in his cravat, the several diamond and sapphire rings, the large, chased-silver buttons inlaid with sapphire chips.

"Savernake, you are a flashing cove today," the viscount observed, sipping from his wineglass.

Savernake looked at his fingers modestly and touched his cravat. "You refer to my acquired wealth. Why, yes, I do believe I shall live comfortably and well from now on."

Cerestone rose slowly, putting his glass aside. "She is not yours yet," he said softly.

Savernake laughed. Heads turned. Several newspapers rattled and hushing noises sounded like hissing pipes. "How charming! Do you propose to challenge me, Cerestone?"

"I would not wish her name linked with yours."

"It already is, I'm afraid. You really should back off like a good fellow. You have lost. At least have the grace to bow out when you are soundly defeated."

Cerestone relaxed his fists and began to smile. "One should play one's cards closer to the chest, Savernake."

"What mean you by that?"

"You have handed me the game."

The dark eyes narrowed, but the manner was studiously languid. "You merely bluff, my dear fellow."

"The game is not over until one player withdraws," the viscount said, a happy gleam in his green eyes. "And I will never withdraw."

"How fatiguing. You are a fool."

"Better a fool than a dilettante."

"I take exception to that."

"Good."

"But I shall allow it to pass. You see, the winner is magnanimous."

Cerestone's smile was awful. "Look to your hand, Savernake. I have you now." Obviously Savernake had extorted money from Lady Alianora—money, gambling, Savernake, Percy, Alianora's brother . . . Yes! Now he understood the hold Savernake had over Alianora. *Marry me or I'll see your brother jailed for debt.* Savernake, the Captain Sharp, must hold all Percy's vowels.

They stared at one another for a long moment until Mr. Raggett begged them to desist. Never mind that the exchange had already generated a dozen wagers being even now recorded in the betting book; he could not allow it to descend into a brawl and so led Lord Savernake to the card room insisting that the play was especially skillful and deep this evening. Cerestone sat down. His friends leaned forward. They agreed with his conclusions and together the three of them worked on a plan to save the Lady Alianora. Cerestone remembered that Trench had a shady cousin, Carnaby, part-time Bow Street Runner . . .

Dear Katie. Despite her occasional weak spells, she dragged Alianora to routs and balls, determined to introduce her to the entire tribe of eligible bachelors. Alianora went through the motions, dancing, conversing, surprised to find herself the object of compliments and friendly overtures. Perhaps she should not judge the modern world on one incident or one person. All this new attention did not, however, lessen her pain or make it bearable.

She saw Lord Cerestone often when he escorted his sister and the Finsburys to various entertainments, but he did not come near her. Lord Savernake seemed to have disappeared, for which she was grateful. He would be arranging for her brother's safety.

She became quite absentminded, missing whole conversations, rarely noticing who solicited her hand for a dance. That is, until Lord Cerestone suddenly drew her up from her reverie and into a waltz. She turned to flee, but he merely tightened his hold.

"Running from me would be cowardly, my lady," he said with no smile.

She lifted her chin, meeting his eyes. There was no softness in them.

"Then I shall face you," she said.

"Yes. I begin to think you are too brave, however. Facing all the dragons by yourself can be fatal."

"You are the only dragon I am fighting. You are the one who insists on telling me what I must do. *I* decide what I shall do," she told him.

Lord Cerestone was silent, realizing he'd heard almost the same words from his sister. And his impulse was the same as then—he wanted to say, "You are too young," but let the words go unspoken this time. This was an intelligent, caring young woman in his arms, one who would give what she had for others, but when it came to herself she lost all perspective. Someone had to help her. He would interfere just this one last time and then back away forever if that was what she wished.

"You may still call me Peter," he said softly, swinging her to avoid a couple who seemed oblivious of other dancers.

"If I choose," she insisted.

"If you choose, certainly," he allowed, thinking that he was making a tremendous concession and that he really didn't mind. But then he thought of this beautiful, loving creature in Savernake's hands and he grew angry, and asked, "When shall you wed Lord Savernake?"

She stumbled. He pulled her closer. She stiffened as he whirled her through the french doors and out onto a dark terrace, trapping her against the stone balustrade.

"When?" he demanded.

She shook her head, pushed at him. "Please, my lord, someone will see us. I must return."

He was immovable. "You will not marry Savernake." He couldn't control his temper any longer. Placid Peter he was not.

"I must," Alianora said. "You do not understand."

"Yes, I do. You think far too much of others—Fanny, your brother, your sister-in-law, your father, your hawks. When will you consider yourself?" His voice grew hoarse.

"I do consider myself. I am not happy unless those about me are happy."

It would make his plan so much easier if she would give him a time, a place. Savernake would never marry her openly, knowing her elder brother would object. "Does it mean nothing then that you are making me unhappy?"

"It means—it means too much, I think," she stammered. "Please, stop. You are torturing me."

He let his arms drop. "It is not I who am destroy-

ing you. I only wished to love you. Here is proof."
He picked up her hand, placed something cold and
hard in the palm, then closed her fingers over it.
"Part of a promise that you shall not wed that libertine, an item retrieved from a pawn shop."

She closed her eyes and when she opened them,
he was gone. Soon, very soon, it would be done and
she would be back at Grassmere sinking into its
comforting embrace. Her brother would be safe and
Lord Savernake would be somewhere else, enjoying
what was left of her portion. And she need never
see Lord Peter Cerestone again.

Relaxing her fingers, she looked at what he had
laid in her hand.

"Oh, my Lord," she whispered.

It was the sapphire necklace Katie had given her,
which she had handed over to Lord Savernake. That
would mean Lord Cerestone must have followed
him, that he might have discovered everything
about her brother, and that he truly meant his parting words. Part of her wished he could ride in with
sword and lance and win the queen of love and
beauty; part of her feared for his life. Now there
was even more to worry about.

With little sleep behind her, Alianora went riding
in the park the next morning for her customary
meeting with Fanny, hoping that she would not encounter Lord Cerestone. Emerging from the elms,
she saw Miss Tavisser and greeted her, expressing
the hope that she was completely recovered.

"Why, yes." Miss Tavisser nodded. "A minor
thing really. If you'll see to Fanny, my lady, I'll just
take Bobbin and Hector over there where they both
might run."

Alianora agreed and joined Fanny. The little girl looked as if she might burst. Her brown eyes sparkled.

"I have a surprise! Alianora, watch me!" she insisted and began to push down on the arms of the chair.

Alarmed, Alianora held out her hand but Fanny shook her head, saying she would do it all herself. She then stood, wavered a bit, the white muslin dress settling neatly on the tops of her tiny boots. Concentrating, she took one step, then another. Alianora bit her lip then opened her arms as Fanny reached her.

"What a lovely surprise!" she said lightly, tears starting in her eyes. She touched the soft brown hair.

Fanny looked up at her. "I must also tell you that we are to leave tomorrow."

Alianora stood still.

"Peter will escort us, of course. Mama and Georgy will stay in town to prepare for the wedding."

"Yes, I had heard she was to wed Buck Rasherly," Alianora said distantly, stricken by the idea that Lord Cerestone would be gone. Had she truly believed that somehow—? Perhaps she had. Now there was no hope at all.

"I must sit down," she said at last and Fanny joined her on the bench.

"Are you sickening for something, Alianora?" Fanny asked in concern. "You do look awfully tired. I know it is not a polite thing to say."

"It is quite all right. And, yes, it is true. I find I do not sleep well in the city."

Fanny considered this. "There are many exciting

things to see in the city, but I prefer the country too." She frowned. "I shall see you again, shall I not?"

"I certainly hope so!" When that might be, she could not say.

Fanny bit her lip a moment then spoke quickly. "Shall you not be marrying Peter then?"

It surprised her. "I—I cannot."

"Why? I know he loves you. He tells me ever so many stories about you and about Grassmere."

"Does he?"

"And I should like most of all to meet your hawk. I have never seen one but in the sky. Does it not hurt to carry it on your wrist?"

"I wear very thick gloves," Alianora told her.

"Do you not love him?" she asked in ambush.

Alianora could not dissemble before the wide brown eyes. "Yes, I do." It was surprisingly easy to say. A feeling of warmth swept through her not entirely due to the emerging sun.

"Then you must be married."

"How I wish life could be that simple, sweeting. Peter might be able to explain it all to you."

The lower lip quivered. "What you are saying is that I never will see you again."

Alianora touched the fine-boned cheek. "We shall see one another, that I promise. And to make certain of that, I shall lend you my psaltery until we meet again."

Fanny reached for the purple velvet-wrapped instrument. "Oh, truly?" Then she sank back. "Oh, but Peter would never allow me to borrow such a fine thing."

"If he objects, have him speak to me. You may

practice all you wish. I shall expect some fine plucking when next we meet."

Fanny looked thoughtful. "But if you were to
marry Peter—"

"That is not possible, sweet *burde.*"

"Is it an evil baron?" Fanny asked anxiously. "Peter has told me just such a story. But he was able to
challenge him in combat and pulverize him."

"Pulverize?" Alianora asked faintly.

"Well, it was all in a story, and perhaps not pulverize precisely, merely run him through."

"Yes, in stories the hero always defeats the villain, but in real life I'm afraid the endings are not
always so neat."

Fanny looked wistful. "I wish they might be."

So do I, thought Alianora. Aloud, she said, "Shall I
teach you one more song to take with you?"

"Oh yes, please do."

And the two of them sat for a comfortable half
hour until Miss Tavisser said it was time to leave.
Alianora rode away from them feeling quite bereft.

Time seemed to pass too quickly and yet not
quickly enough, Alianora thought as she answered a
cordial note of apology from Jane Finsbury and an
invitation to her wedding with the Reverend Andrew Colley. Another couple marrying for love. She
sighed. At least she would soon see Percy and see
that no harm had come to him. She sighed again.
Lord Cerestone was gone now, back to Woodhurst
and his history studies. She imagined Fanny dancing like a fairy on the lawn when she recovered. The
thought made her smile.

"That *man* is here again," Mrs. Bowman said with
an expansive sniff as she entered the drawing room.

Alianora looked up from the desk. "Thank you, Mrs. Bowman. I shall go below directly."

The older woman's look beneath her lace cap was eloquently disapproving, but she said nothing, having learned that Alianora, for all her quiet ways, was quite stubborn. It did not keep her from watching anxiously out the window as Alianora was handed up into Lord Savernake's curricle.

It was another of his "puff-off" rides, Alianora thought as she sat beside him. He had told her quite frankly that being seen with her improved his credit and his standing with her brother's creditors.

"For if you have no more jewels to pawn or any of the ready then it must be seen that there is potential for future payment," he told her. "Although your brother is still, most unfortunately, in some danger from the bailiffs."

"I have no more to give you," Alianora said with a sigh, watching absently as a small gig passed them.

"The solution then is to be married as soon as possible. With your portion I may settle your brother's debts and continue to live comfortably."

If it were a hundred years from now it would be too soon, Alianora thought as they entered Hyde Park.

"Smile, my dearest," he whispered. "Else people will think me holding you here against your will."

She let the corners of her mouth rise, but her smile did not light her eyes. It was then that she noticed the gig again, noting it for the small driver, a man easily mistaken for a boy but for the withered-apple face. Lord Savernake frowned and told her that *that* was a bailiff—the man had been following him for several days now.

"As surely as you breathe, he is looking to find your brother."

She shuddered but was distracted by the appearance of Buck Rasherly and Henry Parkington, both of whom slowed their horses and rode alongside the curricle.

Alianora congratulated them on their forthcoming nuptials, feeling that it was balm to her wounded spirit that they had not cut her. Her companion, of course, was not pleased. His smile was filled with the cold contempt of a true Corinthian.

"Quite a surprise," Buck admitted to her. "But then my Georgy has blossomed into the veriest rose."

"Yes, you knew her when you were quite young," she remembered.

"Visited Woodhurst every vacation. Hated our old castle in the north," he mused.

The mention of Woodhurst sent a pang through her, but she kept smiling.

"Will you then live in London?"

"My dear, without doubt."

She searched her mind for questions, wishing to keep Lord Cerestone's closest friends by her side for just a little while longer.

"And you, Mr. Parkington, will you live on your estate?" she asked.

He nodded, controlling the sudden caracole of his mount admirably. "First, stop off in Ireland."

"To view his new acquisition, that is, not Lady Morfey but her excellent stable," Buck explained a bit awkwardly as if he were a little nervous.

"When do you plan to be married?" she continued.

"End of the summer, I believe. Miss Everhurst

must have a big, flashy ceremony so we have engaged St. George's for that time. Parkington, here, will simply jump the broom or whatever the Irish do."

Henry looked affronted. "Fine ceremony. Lots of lace," he objected.

"Over the anvil," Buck supplied.

"That would be appropriate for two horse lovers," Savernake observed nastily.

Everyone ignored him.

"You will come, of course," Buck invited. Henry echoed him.

Alianora looked from one to the other. "I wish that I might; however, I—I'm not certain where I shall be." She wanted to ask of Lord Cerestone, but what could they know? He had been gone only a few days.

"Of course," Buck agreed. He held out his gloved hand, a light of concern in his gray eyes. She seemed unusually melancholy, he observed.

She took it, a little puzzled as something hard was pressed into her palm. Buck tipped his hat with a smile and lifted his chin toward Savernake, then he and Henry rode on.

She glanced into her palm held down by the side of the curricle. A Roman coin. *The* Roman coin. The one the viscount and Buck passed back and forth after their war of wits. What did its appearance mean? What *could* it mean? Was it a final token of Lord Cerestone's esteem or a sign of hope? She tucked it inside her glove, hoping that the viscount would do nothing foolish.

"Now that we are rid of the Walking Stick and the Obtuse Horseman—"

"You will not speak of them except with respect for they are my friends," she told him fiercely.

"Ah, now. I only wish I might inspire such fervor. No matter. One finds passion where one might." He leaned a little closer. "I have procured a special license, my dear. The sooner we marry, the sooner your brother may move freely again. Today," he suggested.

"No!" she insisted then moderated it. "I must see Percy first."

His lips thinned. "You endanger him with your delay. Have you heard anything of the miseries of Newgate? Perhaps it is time someone enumerated them for you." He truly did not need to exaggerate to overset her, telling of those forgotten in dank cells who had only rats for friends, who could not afford to bribe guards for a minimum of human comforts including food that went beyond a tasteless gruel; one acquired wretched diseases, the teeth would loosen and fall out . . .

"Stop!" she cried softly. "I—I won't let him go there, you may be sure."

"I am the one to help you save him without doubt. If you still insist on seeing Percy, we must make plans to escape the notice of our dunning friend."

She knew of whom he spoke: the small man in the gig. He then went on to tell her of his strategy, mentioning closed carriages and dominoes and the dark of night then suddenly cried "Ah!" with satisfaction. "There is our fellow conspiratress now."

He drove the curricle to the inner side of the tanbark and stopped. There strolled Miss Cressida Finsbury, a picture of demure femininity, with her maid.

"Miss Cressida," he greeted.

She gave him a coy smile from beneath the poke of her bonnet.

"Lord Savernake, a surprise and a pleasure," she said. "And Lady Alianora," she added as if it were not.

"We have been speaking of the Blackworth masque," he told her.

"Oh yes. I am quite looking forward to it."

"You will be 'round to fetch Lady Alianora at ten. I believe that was the time agreed upon."

"Yes, ten," she agreed.

"My men and I shall distract any followers as you go to the masque. Do not worry if you hear shots."

Cressida laughed. "Such a lark! You are quite an *intrigant,* my lord."

He smiled at that and bowed. "Until then." He flicked the ribbons. "Such an unusual girl, quite prepared to do anything to get what she desires, even Lord Cerestone."

She winced a little at that but now understood Cressida's interest. By helping Lord Savernake elope with Alianora, she would eliminate a rival for the viscount's affection. Cressida and Lord Savernake had certainly been whispering together during the ball at Hurst House, she remembered. Then she wondered—Lord Cerestone could never marry Cressida, could he? Even her own sister Jane thought it a miserable match. He had been so angry and hurt—could he turn to someone like Cressida for support? The thought made her ache. No one noticed that Buck and Henry managed to stay within earshot.

"Of course, you will dress appropriately: a costume, a black domino that I will have sent 'round to you. You should really take a cue from Miss Finsbury, my dear love, and endeavor to please me more."

She looked up at him, her dark blue eyes ice cold. She was becoming rather weary of his managing hand. Perhaps she was marrying him to save her brother, and spare her father from scandal, but she no longer thought she would be such a biddable wife.

"After all, I am quite a catch," he continued with a smile for her that bordered on contempt. "You shall be the envy of many women and that should please you."

What would please her, she thought, grinding her teeth, would be the sight of a long hat pin stuck in the thigh that he pressed against her. And she'd not regret doing it for a moment this time.

Buck lifted his quizzing glass as Alianora and Savernake drove out of the park, fingering the crushed pearl design of the handle. He tapped the glass against his cheek in thought, thinking about what he had overheard.

"Something is afoot," he decided. "What say you?"

"More like something is a-curricle," Henry commented.

"Why, dear boy, how clever," Buck observed absently. He nodded to the small man in a gig as he drove past and out the gate. "Mr. Carnaby will discover it if anyone might."

"Strange man," Henry pronounced.

"But persistent. He is on Savernake like a terrier. We'll keep her safe until friend Cerestone's return. By the by, dear boy, had you heard Cerestone's latest plan? It'll put you in St. Bart's. Pure romantic folly—" He proceeded to explain and had Henry guffawing so loudly that horses on the other side of Rotten Row shied from the noise. Parkington choked, wiping his eyes.

"Armor! Wish I might see it!" he said fervently.

"We must be content with only the report," Buck sighed and they proceeded out the gate.

Alianora arrived home to discover that the worst possible thing had happened.

"William!" she greeted blankly, her mind in a whirl.

He kissed her cheek. "Alianora. You do look rather wan, as Katie has been telling me."

Katie stood, laid her hand on her husband's arm and looked directly at Alianora.

"It is the city, as I also said, my love, nothing more," she told him.

Alianora relaxed a little and sat down, removing her bonnet. William could not have seen her arrive with Lord Savernake or he would have said something immediately. William was not a subtle man.

"Did you—did you have a pleasant journey in the north?" she asked.

"Pleasant enough, but it was to be no vacation, purely business. Brought in some new tenants, ousted a few lazy fellows, bought some new animals—all quite normal estate business." He looked down at her. "Have you enjoyed your stay in town?"

"In some ways," she answered carefully.

"Well, no, I wouldn't expect you to take to the city but then the experience is always good," he mused. "But I had hoped you might make some friends, perhaps discover an interesting young man."

No, he was not truly subtle. She smiled at him. "There are any number of interesting young men in town."

"Any in particular?"

"William!" Katie scolded with a smile.

"All right, yes, cease the inquisition, I know, my love. Not even a word about that Savernake fellow since you have ceased to see him. I was wondering, however, about our brother. Have you heard aught from him, Alianora? He was gone from his rooms."

"He did come to visit once," she said, thinking it was safe to admit that.

"He did?" Katie asked in surprise.

"In the afternoon while you were lying down," Alianora told her.

"What had he to say?" William asked. "I know he's been hanging about with that Captain Sharp Savernake. I fully expected to find Percy in the suds when I arrived. Did he come to ask for money?"

"No, he did not ask for money," she answered truthfully. She had given it to him without his asking.

"Did he say where he'd gone to?"

"I believe to a fight or race just outside town."

William nodded. "To be expected, although one might believe he left town to escape the duns. I wish I might know the extent of his debts so that they could be settled before he returns to school."

"I thought you told him you would not advance another penny and would be happy to see him languish in prison," Alianora accused. Those had been his words at Grassmere.

"Ah, said merely to put the wrath of God in him."

"Rather, the wrath of William," said his loving wife.

Alianora was stunned. "Then you would never allow him to go to prison?"

"Do you think me such an ogre?" He chuckled.

Well, yes, she did, at least she *had* thought so.

"No need to let him believe I pay it willingly, however. He should be made to suffer for his follies —but debtor's prison? Never! After all, a young boy must sow his oats."

"No matter the amount of debts?" Alianora was still amazed.

He frowned. "You have heard something."

"No, not specifically, not precisely, that is." She was babbling and stopped herself before she gave it all away. Percy, Savernake, the marriage . . .

"I know you two are quite close so I shall not ask you to reveal anything—as long as he is well."

Alianora nodded. Oh, why was he so understanding all of a sudden? She remembered well how William had shouted at Percy about the gambling losses. Both she and Percy had believed him an ogre. Katie's next words, however, explained all to her.

"Alianora," Katie said, sitting down next to her and taking her hands. "We have something to tell you." She looked up at her husband.

Alianora looked from one to the other, realizing that there had been rather an air of suppressed excitement about them.

"Yes?" she prompted.

"I am increasing," Katie announced.

"Oh," Alianora said, stunned once again, then,

"Oh!" This had been the cause of Katie's "illness." She hugged them both. "How wonderful! Oh, Katie, I feared you were truly ill."

"Far from that," Katie assured her.

"I shall visit our lawyers and then we shall return home to Grassmere," William told her. "I am certain that will make you happy, Alianora." He had resigned himself to the fact that she would find no husband this year and with Katie in need of company, perhaps it was for the best.

Alianora sat silently for a while as William and Katie spoke together, almost cooing. If ever there were a time for Percy to approach William for help it was now. William in a jovial, expansive mood; William revealed as a kindly despot—he would most certainly handle Percy's problems. For her it was too late.

She looked at her brother, his normally stern face bright with happiness, at Katie who could not stop speaking of the miracle—and she sighed. How she envied them!

Chapter Eleven

It required only a little time to ready herself for the masque. She had dressed in just this way every day of her life at New Grassmere—a long plait bound with ribbons, an emerald velvet surcoat, a canary linen undertunic with a topaz ring as the only adornment. Staring into the mirror, she frowned at her appearance—too pale, too sad. The box containing the black domino lay on her bed. She had avoided it all day, feeling as if it contained a coiled snake.

Katie and William had merely nodded when she told them she was attending a ball—no specific one was mentioned—with Miss Cressida Finsbury. It was, therefore, all too easy to walk outside and step into her carriage.

A lamp inside lit Cressida's unsmiling face framed by the hood of her scarlet domino. She was busy looking out the carriage window and barely acknowledged the newcomer.

"Ah yes," she whispered to herself, sitting back against the squabs as the carriage pulled away from the curb. "We are followed."

"We are?" Alianora asked worriedly.

"Quite a brute of a man, really. You need not worry, however," she added with a slow, cold smile. "Richard has all well in hand."

Richard. Alianora could not bring herself to use his Christian name even now on the brink of marriage. Probably not even afterward, she thought wearily.

"I must warn you," Cressida said. "Things may get quite lively before we reach the Blackworths."

And things did. The carriage suddenly jumped forward tossing Alianora to the floor, then against the door, then back on the seat. She finally managed to catch a swinging strap and steady herself.

Unruffled, Cressida laughed. "How clumsy you are. It strikes me as so odd that men are interested in you at all, especially men like Cerestone and Savernake. No conversation, only passable looks, no grace to speak of. For Richard I suppose it is the money. For Peter I truly cannot imagine—he must have temporarily lost his mind."

"One day, Miss Finsbury," Alianora said softly after listening to this stream of invective. "One day you shall poison yourself with such an excess of spleen. Or else someone shall strangle you."

Cressida laughed again. "Too amusing. You must think of me with Peter when you are wed to Richard."

A mace would do quite nicely about now. Alianora leaned forward.

"You must think of *me* in Peter's thoughts when he is with you," she said.

Miss Finsbury's eyes flashed, her face contorted. "I hope Richard beats you well."

"He shall never beat indifferently." Alianora laughed, feeling a strange sort of hysterical control over the situation.

"He thinks you quite stupid and provincial."

"He is ever one for a compliment."

"He loves your money well," Cressida continued, her voice rising.

"Your mind appears to run along one wagon track, Miss Finsbury. How dull it must be for you when there is no company but yourself."

Cressida shrieked. The carriage door opened.

"Cressida, I see you are in fine form this evening," greeted Lord Savernake. He was dressed from hat to pumps in black but for a snowy cravat and diamond stickpin. "We had no trouble eluding your pursuers," he told Alianora.

She nodded, feeling oddly cold and distanced as he handed her out. She had already managed to tie the tapes of her mask and looked about from tiny eyeholes. There were linkboys on the steps to light the way, a noisy crowd in the street shouting at the guests, horses neighing and prancing, and guests pushing past on the way into the Blackworth mansion.

"Is Percy here?" she whispered anxiously.

"One might say so if one were not within earshot of half of London," he warned her then led the two of them into the house and up to the ballroom.

She was struck immediately by how dim the room was. From the entrance where they waited to greet the hostess, she could see many black dominoes interspersed with flames of scarlet and gold, pale blue and lustrous green. It was also quite warm, she noticed, and filled with exotic perfumes.

"Just as I imagined it!" breathed Cressida.

It was like nothing Alianora had imagined. It was like a nightmare filled with faceless demons. She briefly took the hand of their hostess then Lord Savernake pulled her onto the dance floor where a waltz had already begun.

"Shall I see him now?" she asked, careful to mention no names.

"What, escape to a private room already? Quite unseemly, my dear. First we must dance."

The waltz was danced quite differently at this ball. Lord Savernake held her against him, his arm pressing tightly into her back. She endured it knowing that it was the price she must pay before seeing Percy.

And at last Lord Savernake did lead her away, the scarlet domino close behind. They walked down a dark hallway then entered a small drawing room to the left. It was lit by one candelabra on the mantel, the flames throwing flickering shadows over the furniture and across the walls.

"Your sister is here, dear boy," Savernake announced. "We are quite safe, I believe."

A shadow detatched itself from a chair. Alianora removed her mask, put back her hood.

"Percy?" she called softly and was suddenly enveloped in a tight hug.

"Oh, Allie," her brother moaned into her shoulder. "I have made such a mess."

She touched his head. "It would seem so, but it will soon be taken care of, dear brother."

He sighed and raised his head. "I shall never gamble again."

She smiled. "Such rash promises. Perhaps if you were to gamble more moderately."

"That is difficult," he admitted. "One is caught up in the excitement and before the evening's over one might be out a fortune."

"How affecting this is," commented Cressida.

Alianora turned to Savernake. "Please leave us a moment, my lord. I shall speak to my brother alone." It was not a request and he acknowledged her determination with a slight bow. Cressida tugged at his sleeve.

"I have not yet danced and I quite wish to do so, Richard—with you in particular. Such grace!"

He smiled, amusement in his hooded eyes, and led her from the room.

Alianora then pulled her brother to a sofa and sat down.

"Percy, I must tell you something." She quickly repeated her conversation with William.

"So I am to be an uncle again," he said with a laugh. "That *is* good news. I can't wonder at William's sudden goodwill then—but—" He shook his head, pushing back the pale hair that had fallen into his eyes. "He has no notion of what I have done, how much I owe. In truth, I cannot tell you an exact amount myself."

"I believe it truly would not matter now. No one can replace their Robert, of course, but this new baby has lifted his spirits. He seems unusually generous."

"He would have to be to help me."

A little exasperated, she asked at last, "Just how much do you owe?"

He grimaced. "No more than five thousand, I believe."

"Percy! How could you! It is a fortune!"

"You see! I cannot approach William; besides, Savernake, who holds most of my vowels, has been taking care of my debts, with the money you have given him. I do thank you, Allie."

"Lord Savernake has assured me he is seeing to your creditors, but I cannot like this sneaking about."

"There are those who would see me jailed."

"They must be quite unreasonable."

"They make their living fleecing young greenheads like me," he sighed.

"As William has said, young men need to sow their oats. I suppose those oats don't have to be made of gold," she mused.

"I do promise never to throw myself into the River Tick again." He had to explain that bit of slang to her. "And Savernake has been the best of good fellows. Now that you are to marry him he shall always be about to rescue me if I should fall again. You do not mind wedding him, do you? I know that we must all marry sometime and he is not so terrible. I know you have no one else."

She went quite still then reached out and brushed back his hair. "I would do anything for you, dearest brother."

"I know that," he said, then looked closely at her. "You do not seem happy for me or is it this wretched dim light?" It had never occurred to him that she might actually mind, not until now.

"I am worried for you," she said.

"I shall come about. Why, only yesterday I won ten guineas on a carriage race and before that thirty-five pounds on a horse race. You see, my luck is already changing."

She was silent.

"I know, I know. I promised I shall never gamble again and I won't."

"Then promise also that you will go to William."

He looked stubborn. "William will merely stomp about and yell."

"He has said that what you have done is normal, for the most part, and even expects that something like this will happen. Go to him. For my sake, if not yours."

"You are truly worried," he said in surprise.

"I do not wish to see you in Newgate. William does not either."

He looked thoughtful. "I suppose not." Like a little boy, he wanted everything to be taken care of, no matter what horrible things he'd done, but a maturer light came into his eyes as he looked at his sister. Her smiles and laughter seemed forced. He thought of something. "Savernake has not compelled you to marry him, has he?"

"He has not forced me."

"But I know you—and I believe you would be

dancing about the room and singing if it were what you wished."

She then smiled, eyes burning a little. "No, I never could dissemble well, could I? But, as you say, I shall come about."

Percy stood up, agitated. "Savernake gave me to believe you were madly in love with him, that you had *begged* him to marry you."

She looked astonished.

"I had wondered a little on that score," he admitted, embarrassed now by his thoughtlessness. "Forgive me! I've been so obsessed—perhaps it needed this—"

He didn't finish. The drawing room door burst open and slammed against the wall. Three rough-looking strangers rushed in and made straight for Percy. Alianora stood up and tried to place herself between them and her brother, but she was pushed out of the way.

"Bailiffs!" Percy whispered hoarsely.

"Got you at last, young blighter," said a raspy voice. "You play the game, you pay."

Two men grabbed Percy and started to take him from the room with a third man directing them. Percy struggled and managed to cry, "Allie!"

That cry pulled out all her protective instincts and she rushed after them.

"Percy! Wait! You cannot take him. I have money. Our family has money—"

The man following the others ignored her. She reached the door in time to hear him say, "No problem, milord. We'll take him to your place as agreed."

"Quiet!" It was Savernake. "She mustn't suspect as I told you."

She stopped in the doorway, staring at Savernake, who frowned fiercely, staring after the men taking her brother. She started to follow, but Savernake held her back.

"Let me go!" she ordered. "I must stop them! I must get to William!"

"If you follow, they'll take you as an accomplice," he drawled. "Let them take your brother. He needs just such a lesson. It shall be a simple matter to rescue him tomorrow after we are married and I have access to your portion."

Cressida joined them as they reentered the room. She sniggered. Alianora narrowed her eyes, looking from Cressida to Savernake, suddenly recalling the words he had spoken in the corridor. Breath hissed in through her clenched teeth.

"You arranged this," she said softly.

"Arranged what, my dear?"

"You laid information against my brother. You brought the bailiffs here."

"Why should I do that?" She had overheard the conversation! Blast! He lowered his eyelids.

"To force my hand," she answered quite honestly.

"It is all your brother's doing. No one forced the boy to gamble."

"No, but you preyed on his weakness. I see it all now, my lord. You were right. Even Miss Finsbury was right. I *am* stupid and provincial." She was breathing deeply, her face like marble in the flickering light, her eyes cold. "I love my brother and though I am not blind to his faults, I cannot like it when someone takes advantage of him. Or me. You, my lord, are not an honorable man and I believe I must refuse to marry you."

He grabbed her chin and held it, forcing her to look into his eyes. "A pity, really. Fire is quite lovely in a mistress, but one wants a docile wife. Come, we are leaving now. I have the special license by me and a minister waiting at an inn just outside the city."

She looked up at him. "No."

"Yes, my dear bride-to-be."

Alianora heard "This is such a lark, Richard!" just before something crashed against her head and all went dark.

"Welcome home, my lord," said Beeley as he opened the door.

Lord Cerestone removed his hat and gloves and handed them to the butler. "A quick uncomfortable ride. Any messages?"

"A number of them, my lord, arriving quite regularly on the hour today. I have left them with your man."

"Good. Miss Georgina?"

"Readying for this evening, I believe, my lord."

"Yes, of course. I shall be here for supper unless my friends decree otherwise."

"At the usual time, my lord?"

"Yes." He went up to the drawing room where Lady Cerestone greeted him, setting aside her glass of sherry as he kissed her cheek.

"Fanny and Bobbin are settled in?" she asked.

"Happy as grigs. Fanny had first thing to visit her pony."

"She did not ride it, I trust."

"No. I believe Miss Tavisser will see that she does not until she is fully recovered."

Cerestone walked to the sideboard, picked up the decanter, and refilled her glass. He then crossed to the door.

"I am sorry to leave so abruptly, but Trench is holding messages for me."

"Oh yes." She brushed her hand across her forehead. "That knocker has not been still all day."

He bowed and left. He found Trench sitting at his ease before the hearth, an open book in his lap. He shut it and rose at the viscount's entrance.

"Ah, my lord, thought it was you below." He immediately began to help Cerestone off with his coat.

"I returned as quickly as possible. Beeley says that there are messages for me?"

"I should say so. Every hour like clockwork, another one due no doubt any moment now."

The viscount took the sheaf of notes and sat in the chair, glancing through them. All from Buck, all hinting that Something Was About to Happen.

"Anything from Mr. Carnaby?" he asked, studying one note.

"Nothing, my lord."

"Well, I don't know quite what I am to make of this, but my friend Mr. Rasherly seems quite worried. His copperplate is not the most easily read. He's heard rumors that the duns are closing in on Lord Savernake, that Savernake plans something with the Lady Alianora."

"It is a great pity that the Lady Alianora intends to wed such a Greek dealer."

"Not if I may prevent it. Mr. Carnaby has discovered how Savernake led her brother to play too deeply. I believe he holds that over her head. Marry him or her brother goes to debtor's prison! She would choose to save her brother, I know that now." He laid the notes aside and sighed. "I don't believe I shall allow her to sacrifice herself even if I must pay his damned debts."

"A proper hero, my lord!"

"A hero would have handled it more skillfully, I think. Whether she will wed me in the end or no, I must stop this wedding."

"She is far too fine for Lord Savernake."

"A warthog would be too fine. Have Beeley send a message to the Albany and let my friends know I have returned."

Trench left and Cerestone had only begun to loosen his cravat when Beeley knocked at the door.

"My lord, your friends are below. I have put them in the library."

"Ah, that is convenient," Cerestone muttered as he bounded down the stairs in his shirtsleeves.

"A pleasant trip, I trust," Buck greeted, raising a simple quizzing glass to his eye, that glass in one ring with another ring at the end of a short gold stick for his finger. He studied his friend. "How utterly outré of us. You've not even had time to change."

"Never mind." The viscount laughed a little and invited Buck and Henry to some claret, which they immediately accepted.

Henry lounged in a wing chair. "Kept an eye on her. Glad you've returned. Something untoward."

Cerestone sat on the edge of his desk, letting one foot swing. "So Buck said. I was about to send a footman to you—"

Beeley stood at the door. "Yes?" the viscount prompted.

"A person, my lord, at the servants' entrance. He insists you will see him."

Cerestone exchanged looks with his friends. "A small man, weathered face?"

Beeley nodded.

"Then it is Carnaby. Send him up."

Beeley sniffed but obeyed. Carnaby arrived, businesslike in a dark frock coat. He held his hat.

"News, your lordship."

The viscount invited him to continue. The small man told of the night's happenings thus far.

"I set Jagger on 'im, the dimber damber cove. He's as canny as a hound that one, tried to lose 'im, but Jagger ain't no Jack Adams—'e 'as some guts in 'is brains."

"A blessing for your friend. What did Jagger discover?"

Carnaby frowned. "I was coming on to it, your lordship. Your Lord Savernake thinks 'e's lost us, you see, but we ain't rum-headed. We followed 'im to a certain party's address."

"Who?"

"A Mrs. Blackworth."

"One of her notorious masques?"

"Aye, your lordship. She runs a fine nanny 'ouse. Well, up comes your lady, no mistaking the yellow poll, and 'ops on up the steps with the lord. What a hubble-bubble followed that, and no mistake."

Carnaby was then disposed to elaborate how he managed to ensconce himself inside the Blackworth house, how he watched as three infamous bullyboys took Mr. Percival Cheney away.

"Dressed as bailiffs they was, but I rumbles 'em instanter—rum kates from the Rookery, born and bred. Off they goes with the young cub and off then goes the flash cuffin with your lady."

The viscount had been clenching and unclenching his hands. "Lord Savernake took her away somewhere? Where?" he demanded softly.

"Jagger went 'arum-scarum after 'em. I told 'im to send the widdle 'ere."

Cerestone nodded. "And where is the boy now?"

"We 'as 'im, no mistake. Roasted the three devils in their feathers we did."

"Then bring Mr. Cheney here. I'll take care of him." He shook the small man's hand. "Thank you, Carnaby, you've done remarkably well, considering your slippery quarry. You may send your bill to Trench."

The little man bowed and left.

"Couldn't understand a damned thing," Henry complained. "Teach these fellows to speak the king's English."

His friend smiled. "It is the king's English, modified a bit. Some words are simply old, of Teutonic origin; some are remarkable adaptations of Latin."

"Which explains your ability to gather his meaning," Buck said. "Where did you find such a gem?"

"He is a cousin to Trench, although you could never imagine the two were related." Peter then frowned, moved off the desk, and began to pace the Turkish carpet. "He said that Lord Savernake has taken the Lady Alianora somewhere and that one of his cohorts will send word here."

A nerve-wrenching half hour passed before they heard.

"Another *person* to see you, my lord," Beeley announced with obvious disapproval.

The messenger was dirty and weary from a fast, hard ride.

"Stopped by an inn," he told them. "The Sun, a lamb's shake this side o' Holborn."

"I must go," Cerestone told his friends after the messenger left. He called Beeley and ordered his curricle put to.

"Hold, dear boy, you shall not go alone."

The viscount looked at Buck. "This has been coming for some time, my friend. I owe Savernake."

"Must go, dear boy. After all, Georgy! A man must avenge his love."

Cerestone grinned. "Yes, of course. How remiss—"

"Naturally, I shall not fight. I leave the fisticuffs to your capable hands."

The viscount bowed.

"Not leavin' me behind!" Henry insisted. "Good in close quarters."

"What of Lady Morfey—not that I should not be glad of your assistance," Cerestone added.

"Free—she is, I am. No leading strings," he explained.

"Not booted, saddled, or bridled," Buck observed. "Quite civilized, really," he added as if it were a surprise.

Cerestone called Beeley once more and ordered the curricle back and the traveling carriage out. The three of them had just stepped to the door when they were stopped by Georgina's call. She stood on the stairway, dressed for a ball.

"Buck, where are you going?" she asked. "We are to attend the Westbere ball tonight."

Buck raised his glass. "By Jove, Georgy, you are uncommon pretty tonight."

She smiled and blushed and lifted her chin. Peter looked up, amazed at how love had softened and brightened her long, sallow features.

"Why don't you remain behind, Buck?" Cerestone offered.

Buck frowned, an extreme expression for such a fashionable face.

"No," he said seriously. "Honor at stake."

Georgina was at his side. "Buck, you cannot leave me without your escort."

"Sorry, dear love. Must go. Must attend your brother."

Georgina pouted but made no scene. The viscount's eyes widened even more. He clapped Buck on the shoulder. Buck automatically dusted it.

"Amazing," he observed. "Let us go."

"Till tomorrow, my love." Buck bowed over her gloved hand. Henry snorted at the chivalric display.

And they were out the door followed by Georgina's indignant "Well!"

Alianora groaned. Her head hurt, throbbed behind the right ear. She touched it carefully, finding a lump.

She lay in a bed in a room in an inn. She barely remembered the coach ride here or being carried up the stairs to this room, having gone in and out of consciousness. Lord Savernake, where was he? She sat up, moved carefully to the end of the bed. Her loose hair was all atangle; her gown twisted about her. The domino was gone. Her feet were bare. She wiggled her toes. Could she escape barefoot? Certainly, if she must!

A brief wish for Lord Cerestone caused her to

close her eyes for a moment and lean her cheek against the bedpost. It would be wondrous if he might appear and rescue her once more, but Lord Cerestone was home at Woodhurst. She must save herself.

She climbed from the bed, lurched to the door, and had the brass knob in her hand when it turned of its own accord. The door swung open and in the one-candle light she saw Lord Savernake looming like a nightmarish death hawk. He caught her as she lost her balance and pulled her against him.

"How pleasant to see you up and about, my dear love," he said.

"Do not touch me," she warned, throwing back her head so that she might glare at him but succeeding only in looking quite provocative.

"So, the knock on the head did nothing for your temperament." He smiled, his eyes hooded. "We'll have supper now. I would not wish you to faint at our wedding."

"How considerate."

She went below with him, her mind working furiously. She would eat to keep up her strength then would escape somehow before the "wedding." Perhaps when she returned to her room. There was a window there. And if she could not escape that way, did she not have the right to say *no* when the minister asked if she "took this man?"

A headache threatened as they sat down to table. Outside the private parlor she'd noted a large man guarding the door. There was one in the stable with the horses too, she remembered. She would have to avoid them all somehow.

It was not an easy meal. Lord Savernake stared at her with his dark fathomless eyes and chuckled ominously every once in a while. She sipped a little from her wineglass, hoping it was not drugged, and ate from several dishes before her.

"I am relieved to see that you are somewhat relaxed. Wine does wonders for the savage breast," he commented.

She eyed him. "You have not drugged it?"

He laughed at that. "I wish a bride who is awake and able to appreciate my skill."

One might not doubt what he meant.

"You are rather suspicious of me of late," he observed. "I am not such a terrible fellow. I have my vices, but there you are; everyone has something they love to excess."

She rather thought him beyond the normal excess, but then she had no real experience in excesses. They both looked up as a carriage arrived in the inn yard, equipage jangling. An ostler yelled.

"Ah, that must be the minister," said Savernake with satisfaction.

Ah, but it was not.

Chapter Twelve

The door to the parlor swung open.

"Mr. Darby, come in!"

"Why, I thank you, Savernake!"

Savernake growled and stood, his chair falling back. Alianora rose with a cry of delight.

"Peter!"

Lord Cerestone bowed in the doorway, holding out his hand to her. She would have gone to him, but Savernake, quick as a flicker of lightning, grabbed her.

"You will be remaining here, my dear girl," he told her.

"I beg to differ," the viscount challenged, his green eyes glittering.

Savernake's eyes were hooded. "By the by, where are my men?"

"My friends have them trussed up in the stable by now, I should think. If you would unhand the lady—"

"I think not."

"I think so."

Lord Cerestone looked at Alianora as if to ascertain something. "You do not wish to marry this man, my lady?"

"I wish him at the devil," she said with spirit.

Savernake looked surprised. Cerestone took a step closer.

"I will ask again, do you love him?" he asked softly.

She lifted her chin. "I do not. I never did. I know now that he is the arbiter of all my brother's woes."

The viscount relaxed. "There is worse. He has spent all the money you so generously handed him on himself—not on your brother's debts."

Alianora turned to look at her captor. "Is that the truth, my lord?"

He shrugged. "I said that one must appear profitable in order to allay the fears of creditors."

"And, rather than settling one's debts, one runs up more," Cerestone added.

" 'Tis the way of the world," Savernake drawled.

Alianora gasped. "How dare you play so carelessly with others' lives!" She slapped him.

He staggered back, his face dark with anger, his hold loosening. She escaped to Lord Cerestone's arms.

"Your brother is safe," he said. "He has been taken to Hurst House."

"Thank you!" she whispered, tears in her eyes.

"I imagine then that we never did actually lose your men tonight?" Savernake observed.

The viscount smiled. "No, as a matter of fact. The men I hire are far more efficient than the Rookery-bait you find to serve you."

"I do not lose, Cerestone," Savernake warned.

"You have this time. And on several other occasions, now that I think on it." He spoke, of course, of his sister, and several other heiresses Savernake had pursued unsuccessfully.

"I will not lose this time," Savernake amended smoothly.

Cerestone, who had turned to leave, looked back into the barrel of an ivory-handled Manton. Immediately he thrust Alianora behind him.

"I have heard the duns were at your door," he said. "I see that the rumors were correct."

"Give Lady Alianora to me and no one shall be hurt."

"You have surely lost your mind, Savernake. Should you shoot, you shall not escape."

"I would be rid of you. You are an amazingly persistent obstacle to my happiness." There was a wild light in his dark eyes as if he had passed the bounds of reason.

"Let us be reasonable men," Cerestone offered. "Look at the facts. I do not intend to let you take

Lady Alianora. You do not intend to leave without her. We are obviously at a standstill. I, therefore, propose an alternative."

The barrel of the pistol wavered a little and the fanatical light faded.

"And that is?"

"What is closest to your heart—the only thing you will ever truly love: a wager."

His eyes narrowed. "What manner of wager?"

"Any you choose except pistols, for I have none and in any case could not hit the side of a horse at five paces. Why not the turn of a card? The highest card wins the lady. No doubt you have just the thing by you."

"It would be a crime to miss any opportunity for a wager." Savernake laid the pistol on the table and drew out a pack of cards from an inner pocket.

The viscount gently squeezed Alianora's arm. "Since it is the Lady Alianora we are wagering for, why not allow her to shuffle the cards and draw for each of us?"

"My lady," Savernake said as he laid the cards on the table.

She seemed to reach for them but grabbed the pistol instead, backing away, barrel pointed at her kidnapper.

Savernake turned instantly into a coaxing charmer. "Come, my lady, you are endangering yourself with that pistol. Let me take care of it for you. I promise we shall work things out amicably. You know you will not shoot me."

He surprised her by lunging suddenly, but Cerestone was ready for him. He intercepted the lunge and down they both went, rolling over and over.

They knocked into chairs, they knocked into the table as each struggled for supremacy.

Alianora watched in horror for a moment then began to insist that they stop immediately. She waved the pistol, but both men, now on their feet, ignored her. They twisted and turned about so swiftly that she could get no clear aim at Savernake. Finally, she gave up, knowing that he had been right: She could not shoot him, even if he deserved it.

A better choice would be to find Buck and Henry. Lord Cerestone had said they were in the stable. She ran out of the inn, barefooted, into the night calling for the viscount's friends to attend him immediately if they wished him to survive. She knew Savernake's reputation and was afraid. An ostler told her the two men were inside the inn.

She found them in the taproom deep in their own tankards of home brewed. Having executed their part of the plan successfully, they celebrated. Both were alarmed, however, to see Alianora fly into the room all muddied, disheveled, and wildly waving a pistol.

"Save him!" she cried.

"Save whom?" Buck asked, rising, his two-ring glass to his eye. "My dear lady, perhaps you had better sit down. You seem quite overwrought." The glass focused on the pistol.

"Please, I fear that Peter will be killed!"

There was a loud crash from the parlor.

"You must go!" she begged.

Buck looked amused. "No need to be afraid. Our friend Cerestone is quite renowned for his skills as a fighter."

The pistol dropped. "He is?"

"Oh yes, dear girl." Buck guided her to a bench despite the glowering glances of a few patrons who did not approve of women in the taproom. When Buck offered tankards for all, however, the sullen atmosphere lifted, became quite jovial. The good boniface was informed that all damage would be paid for and he joined in the mirth.

Alianora, feeling not a little stunned and weary, laid the pistol on the table. She looked at Buck as if he were mad.

"Do you not care if Peter is killed?" she demanded.

"Indeed, care a lot," Henry chimed in. "Thing is, we're not to interfere. His words. Do our part then wait."

"It all began when we were boys," Buck began, settling into his story. "Cerestone read this tome on Greco-Roman wrestling. Ah, well, then nothing would do but he must try out this hold and that one until he simply couldn't be beaten. Marvelous to wager—"

Cerestone and Savernake suddenly reeled into the taproom, fell across a table near the door, scattering tankards, pewter plates of food, and patrons.

Alianora rose. "Oh, no!"

Buck and Henry quickly took advantage of the situation, laying wagers right and left, even trying to bring Alianora in on it, but she refused. She could not bring herself to enjoy this pugilistic display. She did watch, however, as Lord Cerestone whipped Savernake around, got a hold on his neck and slowly choked him.

"No!" she cried and the viscount let go. Savernake wilted slowly. No one moved to catch him.

Buck was the first to congratulate him. "Bravo! Good match, dear boy." He inspected the limp form on the less than pristine floor.

"He has some skill," Cerestone allowed, looking quite disheveled but happily triumphant. He joined them. "You need not have worried, Alianora," he told her. "I know the precise moment to release my opponent."

"I—I was worried," she said softly.

He smiled, a light of great tenderness in his eyes. Taking her hand he brought it to his lips. "You are free to return home now."

"Yes, I am free." She looked at him.

Buck and Henry happily collected their winnings from those who had foolishly backed the wrong man, then generously offered to pay the damage for such excellent entertainment. Everyone had another round of pints.

"Really should do something about the mess, dear boy," Buck observed finally, noting that Savernake was still peacefully asleep at their feet.

A light of challenge lit the viscount's eye. "I have wrestled with the problem."

"He went down in history," supplied Buck.

Cerestone held up his tankard. "Shall we now carry him out on arrack?"

"No. A small beer," Henry answered, raising his tankard.

"Oh," the viscount said, looking at him in surprise.

"Oh," said Buck, swiveling the glass to his friend.

"Oh!" cried Alianora, who then reached into her reticule. She held up the Roman coin. "Here, Henry. I believe this should be yours now."

The others laughed and toasted their friend.

Henry accepted it with a proud bow. The patrons grunted at the strange behavior of the Quality and Savernake groaned.

"A most proper response," the viscount observed, pushing at Savernake with his foot. He then stood, paid their bill, including damages and Buck's generous rounds of drinks, and bowed to Alianora.

"Home, my lady. Your carriage awaits."

The return trip was quick and uneventful. Lord Cerestone bowed her into Katie's house no later than if she had been attending balls all evening. After all that had happened, she doubted sleep would come but stayed awake no longer than it took to lay her head on the pillow.

Percy arrived the next morning quite contrite, confessed all his gambling sins to William without mentioning anything of Savernake and Alianora. Alianora listened at the door and sighed in relief. William was still unusually jovial and, with only a few stern words, said he would pay the outstanding vowels.

And, thus, it was as if the whole incident with Lord Savernake had never happened.

As if—Alianora sighed when they returned to Grassmere the following week. As if she had never been forced into an unwanted engagement; as if she had never met Lord Peter Cerestone.

It was easy to fall into her old life once more—as if she had never gone to town. That was, outwardly it was easy. She visited the mews, took Belisande and other hawks out for training flights. She exercised Geoffrey and the hunting spaniels. She played at prisoner's base with the gardener's children. Her father joined her in riding once in a while, visiting

Old Grassmere to relive valiant battles, and sing good old ballads.

Percy was so humble and good that he began to be a nuisance so William allowed him to visit some of his school chums for the rest of the summer.

Alianora spent a deal of time beneath her willows, reading books of myths and fables and yet comprehending nothing as her mind wandered away to thoughts of a wrestling historian. No matter how busy, how diverted, all thoughts returned to Lord Cerestone in the end as if he were the focus of her being rather than Grassmere.

A number of weeks passed with no word. She felt restless and unhappy. The viscount had once proposed to her. Was he now so disgusted with her that even friendship was out of the question? It was so surprising how life could change in a short time. Life at Grassmere no longer satisfied her. She wanted Lord Cerestone, wanted to marry him, live where he wished to live without a backward glance. He had said he loved her, did he still? Was she too caught up in dreaming now to face reality—the reality that she might never see him again? The thought sent tears falling from her eyes.

A note arrived from Fanny, written in a very carefully formed copperplate. Her skill on the psaltery had improved; she was riding her pony again. She mentioned her brother and Alianora's heart beat faster. Lord Cerestone had returned to Woodhurst but was acting quite strangely. He would ride away from the house and be gone the entire day, saying that he had to "practice" something until he had the knack of it. No one knew what it was. Fanny closed with a plea for her friend to come visit soon and teach her more songs for the psaltery and to write even sooner!

Alianora smiled. She would love to see Fanny once more, but could she bear to see the viscount if he did not wish to see her? Or worse, see him and a new wife if he chose to marry someone else? Just how strong was she?

The Countess of Wynyate joined her son in the morning room, allowing him to serve her her breakfast muffins and coffee. Katie came down from her room and wandered over to the sunshine streaming in the glass terrace doors.

"I see Alianora is already about," she observed, watching as her sister-in-law stopped by the riverbank and dismounted. "Not even in town did she ever acquire the habit of sleeping late."

"Town has changed her in many ways," the countess observed. "Some of them not precisely happy, but she was always one to rise with the birds."

"I am afraid that town engendered some discontent," Katie said. "I truly believed her to be in love with a certain viscount."

"Perhaps that is it then." The countess nodded. "Perhaps we shall hear from him."

Brunson coughed in the doorway and announced that there was a certain knight errant there to see the earl.

The three of them looked at each other in surprise.

"Knight errant?" William asked.

"His words, Mister William," Brunson told him.

"It may be something to do with our harvest home festival," the countess decided. "Your father is busy planning it now. The earl is in his study, Brunson." The butler bowed and left.

Katie ate a light breakfast for she was at that time when food could set her stomach quivering in the morning. She had just finished her coffee when William, about to leave and walk to the stables, called his wife and his mother to the terrace doors.

"Come quickly, see this. Most amazing."

The two women joined him. Katie gasped.

"I know him! That is Lord Cerestone. I was just speaking of him," she added softly.

They watched as Lord Cerestone, dressed in chain armor covered by a white surcoat emblazoned with a green and yellow device, rode straight for Alianora. She sat in the grass with Geoffrey grazing nearby.

Alianora was wondering if she should attend Buck's wedding, which was to be the following week. The viscount would, no doubt, be there. She laughed a little, relaxed back on her elbows, and watched a flock of birds fly over the river. Jane Finsbury had written to say that Cressida had eloped with Lord Richard Savernake. The two certainly would make a charming couple, she thought, remembering how they did seem to have an odd sort of rapport. At least she need fear him no longer. Geoffrey nickered and she looked back. She pushed to her feet in amazement.

"Peter!"

He was the embodiment of a medieval maiden's dream: a knight who rode boldly toward her, handsome with the wind whipping his dark hair, a helmet tied to his saddle. In his arm he cradled her psaltery. Stopping his horse by her, Lord Cerestone bowed in the saddle.

"Well met, my lady."

She laughed. "Well met, indeed, my lord. How skillfully you ride!"

"Why, I thank you. I have been practicing for weeks."

Fanny had said her brother disappeared to "practice" something. So this was what it was. He struggled a little to lift his leg over the pommel and jumped to the ground, even managing to land on his feet. He looked quite pleased with himself.

"Fanny ordered me to bring your instrument to you," he said, placing the purple-wrapped burden in her hands.

She laid it on the grass. "How is Fanny? I received a note from her and she seemed in good spirits."

"Indeed, she thrives." He moved a little closer and smiled down at her, his green eyes tender. "I believe you had much to do with her recovery. Your kindness and attention, your lovely voice and psaltery, all gave her a reason to live."

"Your love and attention mean everything to her," she said.

"And to you?" he questioned, admiring the way the sun lit up her long golden hair, the way her eyes seemed to hold the deep blue of the horizon in them. She looked down and away at his words, focusing on her psaltery.

"Is that why you came, my lord, to return my paltry psaltery?" An imp of a smile twitched at her lips.

He took her hand. "Say *Peter*, please. And no, I have come for this."

Her smile widened. "My hand, Peter, please?"

He laughed. "Yes. Oh yes. Now, if I am only able to lower myself—" He slowly bent his knee, new leather straps and buckles creaking, chain mail chinking, and swayed a little until the knee hit the ground.

"Did you not practice this part?" she asked, eyes wide.

Huffing with the effort, he shook his head. "Somehow, thought it would come naturally."

"You did quite well."

"I thank you again. Now, while I am here in this precarious position, I must say something." She prompted him with her musical laugh. "Ah, I have only just spoken with your father and he has given me his consent. I now ask you please, Alianora, my love, to honor me by becoming my wife before my knee gives way entirely. I shall love and cherish you forever."

Her eyes danced. "This is so sudden, Peter, please. I must have some time—"

His head drooped and he groaned.

"I did not say how much time precisely and, as I would not wish my future husband to injure himself, I shall answer quickly and succinctly: Yes."

"Praise Saint George!" He rose with her help and took her into his arms, kissing her forehead, her eyes, just touching her lips. "Tomorrow, by special license."

She sighed, a sigh that was echoed by a trio of watchers in the morning room.

Lord Cerestone regretted only one thing as he kissed Alianora gently, then passionately. Now he would never see Trench without his fine caracalla wig! But that was one bet he was happy to lose.

Reading—
For The
Fun Of It

Ask a teacher to define the most important skill for success and inevitably she will reply, "the ability to read."

But millions of young people never acquire that skill for the simple reason that they've never discovered the pleasures books bring.

That's why there's RIF—Reading is Fundamental. The nation's largest reading motivation program, RIF works with community groups to get youngsters into books and reading. RIF makes it possible for young people to have books that interest them, books they can choose and keep. And RIF involves young people in activities that make them want to read—**for the fun of it.**

The more children read, the more they learn, and the more they **want** to learn.

There are children in your community—maybe in your own home—who need RIF. For more information, write to:

RIF
Dept. BK-3
Box 23444
Washington, D.C.
20026

Founded in 1966, RIF is a national, nonprofit organization with local projects run by volunteers in every state of the union.

GOLDEN HEART AWARD
from the
Romance Writers of America

Joan Overfield

The Prodigal Spinster

Sara Belding has her life all figured out and that's exactly why she *doesn't* need her pompous older cousin, who wants to see her properly wed! But with the same determination he used to defeat the French, Lord Mallingham sets about the matchmaking as if it were a military campaign he's bound and determined to win—even if he has to marry the girl himself!

ISBN: 0-517-00092-X   Price: $2.50